A LONG WAY FROM WELCOME

A Long Way from Welcome

A Mystery in Paris

Echo Lewis

BETHLEHEM BOOKS · IGNATIUS PRESS

© 2002 Echo Lewis

Maps of church by Joanne Dionne; of Paris, by Echo Lewis

Front cover art © Paul Casales
Back cover and interior art by Roseanne Sharpe ©2002 Bethlehem Books
Cover design by Davin Carlson

First Printing May 2002

ISBN 1-883937-64-7
Library of Congress Catalog Number 2002102849

Bethlehem Books • Ignatius Press

10194 Garfield Street South
Bathgate, ND 58216
www.bethlehembooks.com

Printed in the United States on acid-free paper

CONTENTS

1. "My Kingdom For a Horse!"   1
2. Clues   6
3. Showdown at the Supper Table   13
4. Exile   20
5. Paris   26
6. Beginnings   39
7. Secret Allies   45
8. Trouble Brews   56
9. Detectives at Large   65
10. The Dripping Umbrella   76
11. La Boulangerie   87
12. Between the Walls   92
13. Fake or Mistake?   101
14. The Empty Room   105
15. Tap Dance into Trouble   114
16. Telltale Footprints   127
17. Frère Jacques to the Rescue   134
18. Midnight Banquet   144
19. Trapped!   156
20. Time Runs Out   161
21. Clamor in the Courtyard   169
22. The Last Pieces of the Puzzle   172
    Historic Note   181

ACKNOWLEDGMENTS

Many people have helped with the background accuracy of this book. I especially want to thank Joanne Dionne, Jeanne Guillemette, Teresa Reilander and Reggie Matthews for their advice and assistance in this realm.

While writing *A Long Way from Welcome*, and communicating long-distance with the editor, I had to make some drastic work changes. For her instruction and heroic patience in helping me make the transition from typewriter to computer, I owe a big debt of gratitude to Bonnie Staib. I also want to thank David Malkovsky for his frequent generous and expert computer assistance.

Ongoing thanks go to the members of my Madonna House family, particularly those in Combermere, Paris and Raleigh, for allowing me access to their translating skills and allowing me the time and freedom needed in progressing through the many time-consuming stages involved in the writing of this and other works.

As with any other creative process, writing hits the inevitable moments of discouragement and questioning. For their inspiration, encouragement and moral support at key moments, Michael O'Brien, Christopher de Vinck, Richard Payne and Pat Broderick deserve a big thank you.

Special thanks, too, go to the members of Bethlehem Community for their encouragement and support in fostering the work of Christian authors writing for children and young adults.

DEDICATION

For
Andrew and Alec McQuillen
Bonnie Staib, Jim Guinan
And
Pat Broderick

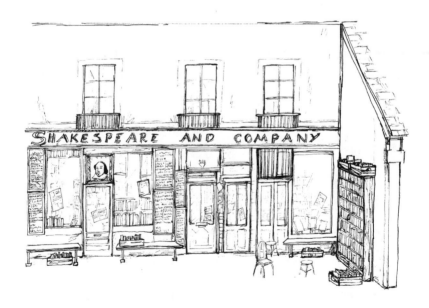

1

"My Kingdom for a Horse!"

ALERT AND PURPOSEFUL, Maggie McGilligan approached her bike as a warrior would a respected opponent. Keeping her eyes on the overloaded front basket, she took a deep breath, gripped the chest-high handlebars of the rusted, crusted relic, and strained to drag the beast away from the school stand.

"'A horse,'" she groaned, pulling at the blue metal monster, "'my kingdom for a horse!'"

"Will you cool it with the Shakespeare, dummy? Keep it up, and I'll never tell you what I found out in Dad's office last night." Tanya Becker, as tall and trim as Maggie was short and tending toward chunky, jumped onto her new-millennium mountain bike and sped across the smooth black asphalt of the Henry Rumbleton Middle School parking lot. Her raven hair flowed out like a river behind her.

"See if I care what you found out!" Maggie yelled into the growing distance between them. "And, hey, thanks for the help!" She yanked fiercely at her bike, and the sleeping Mammoth jerked backward, awake at last. Gripping the handlebars, Maggie jogged along beside it to get it going and hopped on. She slid from side to side on the frayed leather seat, pumping hard to gain momentum.

At the far end of the parking lot, Tanya stopped to gather her long hair into a ponytail, and Maggie, glad for her out-of-the-way braid down the back, caught up—and kept going.

1

"To Finch's and freedom!" she shouted. "Last one there's a duck!"

"Eat dirt!" Tanya leaped back onto her shiny-red wonder-bike, and Maggie was doomed. As hard as she pedaled, she couldn't match Mighty Mammoth to Red Flash. Tanya caught up easily and reached the end of the block half-a-wheel ahead.

Maggie pedaled faster, but stopped caring who had the lead. She let the hot breeze of this Wednesday in June draw her into summer sun and freedom, and toward the railroad tracks that cut across town two blocks ahead. She could hear the seventy-car, two-engine freight to Chicago gathering momentum as it pulled out of the station yard. The engineer Maggie had known all her life would have taken over at the helm.

"Clackety-slap, clackety-slap! Chug, chug, chah, chug!" Maggie's feet left the pedals as she tap-danced the train rhythm in the air. The high school kids claimed that Savion Glover was the best tap dancer in the twenty-first century, but that was only because Maggie hadn't started her lessons yet.

"Clackety-clack, yeah, keep track! Clackety-clack; don't send me back! School's out, and so am I—call me a bird that's flyin' high!" Improvising at the top of her lungs, Maggie dropped her feet back to the pedals and churned toward the track, where the big-nosed locomotive pulled into sight from behind the defunct water tower. Maggie waved to the engineer. "Yo, Mac, go Mac, that's my man!"

The train whistle blasted hello, and Mac's arm appeared in greeting through the engine's open side window before the front end of the train swung north and out of sight behind the lumberyard.

Maggie pulled to a stop beside Tanya at the train track, where they had to wait for the rest of the train to pass. The wait gave Maggie time to jump off her bike and tap the train rhythm on the pavement. Using Mighty Mammoth's handlebars as ballast she did a few high kicking leaps between taps. "Yes, train, go train, sing me free. I love my town, and it loves me!"

"You are utterly crazy." Tanya had to keep one hand on her bike, but she held her other one over her ear. "I'm going to tell your mother to think it over about letting you take tap dancing lessons," she muttered, and as soon as the end of the train reached the intersection, she rolled Red Flash under the rail and escaped around the caboose to the other side of the tracks.

Maggie laughed, ducked under the rising guardrail, got Mighty Mammoth going, and hopped on. Bumping across the tracks, she thanked her lucky stars it was the train heading to Chicago and not her. She shuddered at the thought of the smog, the noise, the lonesome, hollow feeling of being surrounded by strangers. If Maggie ever had to tap dance a city, she didn't know what she would do. Jackhammer and car-horn rhythms meant nothing to her. In order to dance, she needed the rhythmic throb of harvest machinery at Smith's farm, the chattering and scolding of squirrels in Warden's woods, the little kids splashing and yelling at Moody's pond. Shaking the grim picture of city life out of her head, Maggie pedaled hard down the street.

Two blocks past the train tracks, she urged Mighty Mammoth up the curb and onto the sidewalk, where she skidded to a stop between Tanya and the Finch's Bakery storefront. She kicked her stand down and flung the bakery door open before her friend, the unanimously elected princess of the eighth grade, had quit fiddling with her wind-blown ponytail.

"Hi, Mr. Q!"

Jacob Quinnell, present owner and operator of Finch's, stared at Maggie through the upper part of his bifocals. "Where's the fire?" His raspy voice sawed the air. "The way you two landed, I thought we'd lose the window this time for sure."

"Aw, we weren't even close." Flushed and breathless, Maggie grinned up at him.

Tanya appeared beside her at the counter. "I'll take one lemon-filled donut," she said, all business, "along with a cream puff and a diet cola."

Mr. Q's stick-thin hand halted in its reach for a white paper bag on the shelf behind him. "You've got to be kidding. About the diet cola, that is."

"No, I'm very serious." Tanya pulled her freshly brushed ponytail over her shoulder and twisted the end around her fingers. "We're celebrating the last day of eighth grade, but I don't want to get fat."

"Well then, how about a sugar-free yogurt instead of the cream puff?"

"Ooooh, no, I love cream puffs."

Maggie laughed at Tanya's moon-eyed expression, but Mr. Q hung onto his wrinkled frown. He gathered Tanya's order, handed it over, and turned to Maggie.

"I want a double chocolate donut, a maple dip one, and a diet ginger ale—please."

Behind his glasses, Mr. Q rolled his eyes, but he gave Maggie her order, and she and Tanya ran outside. Tanya plunked her donut bag into Maggie's already-bulging wire bike basket.

"Quick," Tanya said, grabbing her own handlebars, "let's sneak into the Roxy and eat our grub."

"Tanya, no!" A knot pulled tight in Maggie's stomach. "Your dad's boutique—look at it! There are two measly lanes of hardly any traffic separating us from *Fashions'* show window. And your dad's not away in Paris buying new clothes to sell. He's right here in Welcome, Indiana—probably with a pair of binoculars trained on *you!*"

Tanya wrinkled her sculptured nose. "'Course he's here in town. Where would the challenge be if he wasn't?" She paused, her head slightly tilted. "I doubt if he's taken to using binoculars yet," she said thoughtfully, then burst into laughter. "I pulled off sneaking into his office above the store last night, didn't I?"

"Barely! You were lucky he dropped the key outside the door—and what if he'd wanted something from the closet while you were hiding in there?"

"He didn't," Tanya reminded her. "I wish I'd had a few more minutes alone in the filing cabinet, though."

"Why? What did you find? It's something about Bartholomew, isn't it? Tell me!" To heck with pride—Maggie wanted to *know*.

"Wait 'til we get into the Roxy. Come on."

Maggie held back. "How about a picnic out in the woods by the creek instead? In the great outdoors. Why should we have to sneak into an abandoned movie theater to eat a couple measly donuts, when your dad makes enough money at *Fashions* to buy you your own theater, if you wanted it?"

"That's just it!" Tanya pounded a delicate fist against her bike seat. "My dad could buy me whatever I want—*ten* bikes like this, for instance—and leave me alone. That's how it's supposed to work when you're a rich kid, right? Not this time! Dad has to change the pattern. He wants to know where I am every second. *And* who I'm with." Tanya's hand went to her slim hip, and she leaned forward over her bike seat. "So far, we've managed to keep up the false impression he's under that you're an upright and respectable companion. So let's hang onto the image, but not have any chickening out here, okay?"

Maggie quailed under the glare of two blazing onyx eyes until, with a twist of her shoulders, Tanya turned away to steer her bike around the bakery.

"Yeesh!" Hating herself for doing it, but not wanting to refuse her friend, Maggie guided Mighty Mammoth between the bakery and the old closed-down Roxy to the alley. Peering back over her shoulder while Tanya pulled a loaded key ring from her belt bag, Maggie thought ruefully of how Tanya's dad really did believe Maggie was a good influence for Tanya. As if Maggie could influence Tanya to do anything. Well, she *had* gotten Tanya into roller blading instead of playing video games every day after school. That was a good influence, wasn't it? Still, at times like this . . .

"Hurry!" Maggie whispered, as Tanya fumbled for an old-fashioned skeleton key and stuck it into the bottom of the rusted padlock that secured the theater's rickety back door.

"Relax," Tanya drawled, but she hastily clicked the lock open and dumped the key ring back in her bag. In one swift motion, she pulled the door ajar, pushed her bike inside, and leaned it against the wall.

Maggie nearly ran the front tire of Mighty Mammoth up the back of Tanya's legs in her haste to get inside the theater. She shoved the door closed with her foot and leaned her bike against Tanya's.

"Okay!" she panted. "We made it. So, what did you find out about Bartholomew?"

2

Clues

IGNORING MAGGIE'S QUESTION, Tanya left her by the bikes and ran off into the darkness. "Let's have a stage picnic!" she said, and Maggie could hear her clumping up the wooden steps to the platform that all the really old movie theaters used to have.

"Turn on a light, cat-eyes, so I can come too!" The excitement that Maggie always felt in the middle of an escapade with Tanya pushed away her guilty conscience at breaking and entering. Her jitters at being left behind in the dark disappeared, too, when a single overhead light flashed on ahead of her, and she could make out the minimal shapes of the abandoned theater—rows of seats, the stairs, and the stage with its ceiling-high background screen. "That's better. And you called *me* crazy!" Maggie ran up the stairs to join Tanya, already seated cross-legged on the stage floor in front of the screen, her horde of goodies spread out in front of her. Maggie unfolded the top of her own bakery bag and peered inside.

Deadly, of course.

"It's not fair," she said, shifting her gaze from the bag to Tanya. "You have the same number of donuts I do, but in ten minutes I'll have gained a hundred pounds, and you'll have gotten skinnier than you are already. Where's the justice in that, I ask you."

"It's genes, you poor thing." Tanya's words came out garbled up with the lemon-filled, calorie-laden pastry she was already wolfing down.

Maggie pulled out her top donut and stared at it. She tapped the chocolate coating.

"Shall I cancel eating in the interest of vanity?" She sighed, and muttered to the ten extra pounds she carried, "'Oh, that this too, too solid flesh . . .'"

Tanya stopped licking powdered sugar from her fingers. "What did you say? Stop mumbling! You just made some nasty crack about me, didn't you? Tell me what you said!"

Maggie sighed, then, giving way to a sudden impulse, leaped to her feet on the stage, thrust one hand into the air, clasped the other over her heart, and shouted, "'Oh, that this too, too solid flesh would melt, thaw, and resolve itself into a dew!'" She dropped her hands and her voice. "Shakespeare again—Hamlet. Like it?"

"Oh, dry up, you drip."

Maggie suppressed a grin. Tanya-the-beautiful looked positively prune-like when she pouted like that.

Tanya must have sensed Maggie's mirth. She quickly rearranged her mouth and used it to tackle her cream puff and change the subject.

"So," she said between bites, "speaking of drips, how're things with your mom and that no-good Bartholomew?"

Maggie sat back down and bit into her chocolate donut, promising herself she would tap dance and bike off any calories that didn't ooze out of the donut on their own accord when she broke it open. Yep, that should do it. She reached for her ginger ale. "Bartholomew's not no-good," she said. "He's terrific."

That's what Maggie said aloud and she pretty much believed it. But, on the other hand, she wasn't sure herself, sometimes, how she felt about Bartholomew. When he was around, Maggie and her mom couldn't spontaneously run out to a movie. Or go for a long walk—just the two of them. Of course, the three of them did things together, and that was nice, but it wasn't the same comfortable relationship of just Maggie and her mom anymore. Everything was changing. That was hard.

"Mom really likes him." Maggie gulped down a long swallow of ginger ale. "She's got good judgment about people, so I'm giving Bartholomew the benefit of the doubt." She grinned.

"It looks like I'll have plenty of time to make up my own mind about him. They're getting married at a special Mass a week from Saturday."

"A week from Saturday! Oh, no, my dad'll have a fit! He wants that sawdust-eating carpenter to go back to Alaska, or wherever he's from."

"The Yukon. And he's a contractor. Hey!" Maggie returned her pop can to the floor. "About your dad's office last night— did you come up with something to explain the big argument we overheard between him and Bartholomew?"

"I think so." Tanya gazed wistfully at the tiny morsel that was the end of her cream puff. Taking a maddeningly long time to do it, she popped the piece into her mouth, chewed, and deliberately swallowed before saying, "I found three folders in a file drawer—but not in the same filing cabinet that has his Chairman of the Board of Gallery One stuff. That cabinet didn't have anything interesting in it. The juicy folders were in his private, personal locked cabinet." Tanya pulled out her well-stocked key ring and rattled it in front of Maggie with a self-satisfied grin.

"Oh, man, if he ever catches you . . ."

"Not to worry. Anyway, the first good folder had a bunch of newspaper articles about this Thea Ronchetti lady. You know how Dad yelled at Bartholomew about how the last decent painting she ever did was the one hanging on the wall in our living room?"

"Yeah, yeah, go on."

"And you remember how Bartholomew yelled back that she'd only started really painting *after* she'd done that one?"

"Right, okay—so?"

"So, after painting the picture we have, she went from modern stuff to traditional, and I guess Bartholomew likes the traditional type, but Dad likes the modern, and you know what he's like when he's on a roll and has a pen in his hand. Well, he scribbled things like 'Ridiculous' and 'Bunk!' across the articles that said good things about the way Ronchetti is painting now."

Maggie's shoulders slumped. "That could explain the argument okay, but it sure doesn't give any clues about why your dad wants Bartholomew out of town."

Tanya leaned forward over her crossed legs. "There's more. Most of the articles in that folder were by somebody named Art Brandenshaw. He raved on lots about how good Ronchetti has gotten since she became—a nun! Can you believe it! I never knew nuns did stuff like that. You're the one becoming an expert on that stuff. Did you know nuns got to be painters?"

"Heck, no. I haven't heard anything like that yet. Nuns pray. And nurse and teach, maybe. I never knew they did other normal-type things." Maggie retrieved her ginger ale can from the stage floor and took a thoughtful swig. "Hey, do you think maybe your dad doesn't like Catholics? Some people don't, you know. Maybe he's starting to feel surrounded. Maybe he doesn't like Ronchetti's paintings now because she became a nun, rather than because she changed her style. And maybe he wants to get rid of Bartholomew because he's Catholic. Wouldn't that be something?" Maggie stopped drinking and ran her index finger around the rim of her pop can. "Weird. I wonder if your dad won't like my mom or me anymore, either, if we become Catholic, like Bartholomew."

"Oh, gee, yeah, maybe." For once, the Princess of the whole eighth grade looked flustered. "Are you still going through with the Catholic thing? I thought your mom was going to let you decide for yourself."

"Yeah, she is." Maggie shifted her weight and rubbed the back of her neck. "I don't know. Mom said we can take instruction in the fall, when things quiet down and we're more settled. It sounds okay to me, but if it means we can't be friends anymore . . ."

"Hmm." Tanya grinned wickedly. "Maybe Dad's afraid that joining up with the Catholics will become a plague, and that I'll catch it. Wouldn't that get his goat! I'll have to think about that one." She gleefully chug-a-lugged her cola and set the empty can beside her on the stage. She wiped her mouth with the back of her hand.

"Listen to what else I found in Dad's office. That folder of articles was just one part. Folder number two in his private drawer had a bunch of articles about all the painting thefts that have been taking place in Paris over the last few years. Lots of the articles were by this Art Brandenshaw too. Nothing strange there, except that . . ." Tanya paused dramatically.

"What? Tell me, you beast!" Maggie threw a pile of napkins at her.

"The third folder," Tanya said, laughing and gathering napkins from the floor and her lap, "was sort of a continuation of the second one. It had a series of articles about stolen paintings over the centuries—practically a how-to-do-it series. Also by Art Brandenshaw. Dad had 'SUSPICIOUS'—all capital letters— written across the front of the last article." She scrunched the retrieved napkins together and threw them in a wad back to Maggie.

"It was getting dark by the time I got to that folder," Tanya said, "so I put the first two folders away and took the last one over by the window, where I could read without turning on a light. You should see some of the schemes people have come up with to steal a painting! Well, I was really into the last article, about a guy more crooked than Jesse James, when I heard someone coming up the stairs. I threw the folder into the file drawer and locked it. Then I grabbed a piece of paper that had fallen to the floor and hightailed it into the closet." Tanya grinned. "You were right—it's a good thing Dad dropped his key, or I'd never have made it. Now . . ." Tanya straightened her right leg and pulled a little piece of crinkled paper from her jeans pocket. She palmed the paper and held her closed hand out toward Maggie. "Guess what this says."

"Tanya, you're driving me crazy—just tell me!"

"Okay." Tanya slowly opened her hand, and Maggie snatched the paper before her friend could conceal it again.

"'A. B. equals B. Britt.'" Maggie squinted, thinking. "Bartholomew Britt is easy enough, but . . . oh—Art Brandenshaw is Bartholomew!"

"Yep."

"Well, ruffle my feathers." Maggie shook her head, hoping some coherent thoughts about all these discoveries would pop out of it. But she couldn't think at all with Tanya rattling on so fast.

"I'd use one of those names that writers use besides their own, too," Tanya was saying, and then hesitated.

"Pseudonym," Maggie supplied automatically.

"Yeah, pseudonym. I'd use one too, if I were writing about how to steal things. Here's what I think is really up. Dad slapped 'SUSPICIOUS' across that last article—which, by the way, was written a mere ten days ago—because he thinks Bartholomew's a thief—an art thief." Having dropped that bomb, Tanya folded her arms in front of her and sat back, clearly pleased with her own deductions. "Dad wants Bartholomew as far away from his private collection as he can get him."

"That's crazy." Maggie dismissed the idea as soon as she heard it. "Bartholomew might be a little goofy sometimes, but he's no more of a crook than Charlie Brown. Those scribbles of your dad's could mean anything. 'Suspicious' could mean he just doesn't believe the story about the Jesse James guy. Good detective work, though," she said quickly, catching Tanya's scowl. "We'll have to keep that information on tap. But there must be some other reason why your dad wants Bartholomew out of . . ."

The full realization of what could happen as a result of Mr. Becker's antagonism toward Bartholomew hit Maggie with a jolt. "Tanya, listen, the real crunch here is . . . the real crunch here is . . ." Maggie fought to keep her voice steady, "if your dad forces Bartholomew out of town, Mom and I will have to go with him, and my whole life will totally change. It'll be ruined! I'll lose Tara—the only home I ever wanted to live in. I'll lose you. And everybody else in Welcome. What will happen to me?" Maggie cleared her throat. "Can't you talk to your dad—find out what's wrong?"

"Talk to him?" Tanya's arms unfolded, and she threw her hands out in exasperation. "*Talk* to him! Nobody *talks* to my dad! *He* talks—especially to me. Forget it!"

"Oh boy, oh boy, what am I going to do?" Maggie chewed on her lower lip. "I've got to come up with some kind of solution, some way to keep us in Welcome."

Too distracted and restless to sit any longer, Maggie got up and retrieved the bakery bags—her own still had the maple do-nut she hadn't gotten to yet—and the pop cans. "I have to go home. Mom'll be wondering about me, and I don't want the topic of where I've been to come up."

"Hey, don't look so gloomy. Your life in Welcome isn't over yet." Tanya got up too. "How about getting together tonight and watching an oldie-but-goodie? You choose. Plus, even with the wedding so soon, you'll still get to come to the cottage with me this weekend, won't you? As for your mom, you can dazzle her with your final grades, and she won't remember to ask where you've been. Go stand by the door. I'll flip the light off."

Outside the back door, Tanya held onto the bikes with one hand and lifted the lid to the old dented garbage can with the other while Maggie dumped their bags and cans and slid the padlock back into place on the theater door.

"See you tonight," Tanya said, turning Mighty Mammoth over to Maggie. "Dad'll probably want me to stay home, but I'll sneak out my bedroom window and come over to your place. Better enjoy it while we can!" She hopped onto Red Flash and pedaled gracefully away.

Tanya's parting shot and the realization that she had just thrown out her second donut combined to make Maggie feel about as flat to the ground as a beaver's tail. With a grunt of exertion, she headed Mighty Mammoth off in the opposite direction from Tanya.

3

Showdown at the Supper Table

MAGGIE RACED THROUGH the back alleys of Welcome as though speed alone could keep her world from crumbling to dust beneath her. Skidding into her own gravel driveway, she jumped off her bike and propped it against the wooden signpost that declared to the world that the McGilligan home was "Tara." Maggie had painstakingly carved and painted the sign two years ago, after devouring *Gone With the Wind* and fighting fire, drought and dreaded enemies right alongside Scarlett O'Hara to save the heroine's beloved homestead.

Maggie lifted the books out of her bike basket to carry them inside, but paused first in the yard to study the old brick house—her own Tara. What was it about this Raggedy-Ann of a building that was so important to her? It wasn't Scarlett's magnificent southern mansion, that's for sure. But, for whatever reason, Maggie loved every chipped red brick of the three-story structure that, since Nineteen twenty-nine, had served as everything from a maternity hospital to a tourist home.

Mara, Maggie's mother, had bought the shaggy giant when, after the boating-accident death of her husband in Lake Michigan, she had moved from Chicago to start life over again and raise her new-born baby—Maggie—in a quiet, small-town atmosphere.

Maggie had always been glad about that move. She loved not only "Tara," but all of Welcome, its people, its surrounding wooded hill country that she hiked and biked whenever she

13

could twelve months of the year. She never wanted to leave her home, and she would fight like Scarlett to save it, if she had to! But—Maggie's shoulders drooped—how could she, a not-quite fourteen-year-old nobody, stop rich and powerful Mr. Becker from wanting to drive Bartholomew away from Welcome?

Her heart as heavy as the load of books in her arms, Maggie trudged up the back porch steps. She crossed to the screen door, and stopped. Voices drifted through the inside hall from the front end of the house. Her mom and Bartholomew sounded deep in serious discussion.

Maggie opened the screen door and went into the house. Too distracted to clue in to the luscious aroma of baking pizza that wafted invitingly toward her from the oven, she entered the kitchen and put her books on the table. Still only vaguely aware of a treat in the making, she passed through the dining room and living room, stopping only at the archway of the spacious front room that held the grand piano—her mother's pride and joy, and the only thing left from her concert playing days. On the far side of the piano, on its matching black bench, Mara and Bartholomew sat, nose-to-nose, talking so earnestly they didn't even see Maggie at first.

From the shadow of the archway, Maggie gazed quietly at her mother. Mara McGilligan wasn't really pretty. No, the proportions were all off. Her green eyes were too large, her pixie nose too small, her mouth too wide for her narrow oval face. But her thick chestnut-brown hair that fell like ocean waves along her cheeks and down past her shoulders blended her haphazard features into a startling, delicate beauty. Maggie wished she looked more like her. At the very least, she could have inherited her mother's rich brown hair instead of getting stuck with being a peanut-butter blonde. Maggie sighed, and switched her gaze to Bartholomew.

Beside Mara, the new man in their lives didn't look anything like the pictures of Maggie's original father, the slender, dashing, trumpet-playing Joe Simms. Not even close. Bartholomew had trimmed his rangy russet hair and beard, and was neatly dressed in gray pants, white shirt and navy sport jacket, but he looked slightly out of place indoors. He needed his usual jeans and plaid work shirt to look comfortable. A real "Sports and Field" man, Maggie thought. Straight from the Yukon wilderness. Still, he and Mara did fit together, in a rock-garden sort of way—a rugged boulder beside an elegant iris.

"Maggie, darlin', come join us!" Bartholomew's voice boomed across the room. Startled out of her reverie, Maggie stepped through the archway.

Mara smiled. "Hi, honey, what kept you so long after school?" "Tanya and I had a donut to celebrate our last day of eighth grade." Maggie held her breath.

Her mother's smile faded. "I wish you two wouldn't spend so much time together."

"She's my best friend!"

"I know she is, honey. It's just that—well—you get so, I don't know—different—when you're with her. What is it that happens?"

Maggie shrugged. "I don't know."

"Come on, you two." Bartholomew stood and pulled Mara lightly to her feet. "We can discuss all this in the dining room. The pizza's ready."

Maggie grinned, forgetting her troubles for a second. "Lumberjack pizza? I thought so! Too bad Tanya couldn't come for supper." She shot a defiant look toward her mother.

"No time for dueling, girls." Bartholomew stepped quickly between them and guided them each by an elbow to the dining room.

Seated at the table, Maggie happily eyed the concoction Bartholomew brought steaming from the oven. His pizzas should be world-famous. Pepperoni, bacon, black and green olives, fried onions, anchovies for the brave of heart, heavenly homemade tomato sauce, double cheese and a crust to melt in your mouth.

"Maggie, darlin'," Bartholomew said as he dished out a piece for her that crowded the edges of her dinner plate, "my sister Thea could do a grand painting of you today—red blouse, blue jeans, your braid that looks like you've been biking in a windstorm. You look fresh as a Gray Mountain flower."

Maggie blushed, but her mind quickly skidded from Bartholomew's compliment. Thea? That name sounded so familiar. Where had she heard it before? Had Bartholomew talked about that particular sister before?

"I didn't—um—I didn't know one of your sisters was a painter—did I?" Maggie grimaced at the betrayal of her ignorance.

"Oh, Maggie . . ." Her mother sighed, a half-amused, half-frustrated look on her face. "If you would pay the least bit of attention, you'd know a lot more about Bartholomew's family—*your* family now."

"Aww . . ." Maggie squirmed. Her mother was right, of course. In the two years since Mara had met Bartholomew at an art exhibit in nearby Fort Wayne, there had been plenty of correspondence flying back and forth between the Yukon and Welcome, containing piles of family-type information. Her mind on biking trails, tap dancing or some Shakespeare passage, Maggie had never bothered paying much attention when her mother read the letters out loud to her. For the same reason, she hadn't bothered with those kinds of details in the last six months, since Bartholomew had moved to Welcome. So many facts had mounted up about each one of his ten brothers and sisters and all the in-laws, it would have taken a computer to keep track of it all.

"Maggie," her mother said patiently, "try to remember. Thea is the reason nobody from the family is coming for the wedding. It's far too expensive for them to come from the Yukon, Alberta or Nova Scotia twice in two months, so we're going to combine our wedding reception with Thea's big show in August. The Gallery is flying her over for the show, and the rest of us are all able to fit in with that schedule."

"Right." Maggie *did* remember hearing her mom and Bartholomew making some August reunion-type plans that centered around a sister who lived in France. A light clicked on in her brain. "Yes—I've got it! Your sister is the Thea Ronchetti who painted the five-dimension boat picture hanging in the Becker's living room! Tanya and I heard you and Mr. Becker when you got so heated up arguing with each other about her painting style. But . . ." Maggie broke off, trying to get it right. "If Thea Ronchetti is your sister, and a nun, why does she have a different last name from yours? You said you had the same two parents all your life."

"True. Thea was married, darlin', but her husband died several years ago. They had no children. Some time after Rinaldo died, Thea shifted direction spiritually *and* artistically, and five years ago, she became a nun. She's Sr. Clare now, assigned by her Order to live and paint in Paris."

"Wow." Maggie struggled for understanding. "Does Mr. Becker know she's your sister?"

Bartholomew nodded. "Yes. He found that out when I came to Fort Wayne two years ago, to represent Thea in the early negotiations concerning the show she'll be having at Gallery One this August. He was already angry with her about changing her painting style and didn't seem thrilled to be working with a relative of hers. He asked me then if I'd like to turn over my job as liaison to someone else. I said I'd rather stick with it myself, and, since it didn't look as though we'd need much personal contact, I guess he figured he could handle it. Neither he nor I thought I would ever be settling down in this part of the world." Bartholomew smiled a special, mooshy smile at Mara.

Maggie grimaced and took a big bite of crusty pizza, waiting for Bartholomew to pull his attention away from Mara and finish his thoughts about Mr. Becker.

"As Chairman of the Board of the Gallery," Bartholomew continued, "and sponsor for Thea's show, Richard said a couple months ago that he should be the one to handle all the paperwork now. I told him that was fine with me, but even having that much control hasn't changed his attitude toward me or changed his mind about Thea's current style—as you can see from our encounter the other day. He still thinks religion has ruined a brilliant career." Bartholomew rubbed his beard, frowning.

"The fact that I'm Thea's brother explains part of his antagonism toward me," Bartholomew went on, speaking more to Mara than to Maggie, "but not all. I can't believe he'd be so petty as to get even with her by blocking me from getting my contractor's permit here in Welcome. As Chairman of the Chamber of Commerce here in Welcome, he does seem to be wielding his power to try and do just that, but it's hard to figure out what his complaint really is. It's also hard to figure out why he's fostering Thea's exhibit, in the first place, when he's so dead set against the way she's painting now."

Maggie sat stunned. Did Tanya know her dad was actually trying to prevent Bartholomew from being able to work in Welcome? That was lots more serious than . . .

"Maggie!"

Maggie started at her mother's exasperated exclamation. "Bartholomew has asked you twice now if you want a glass of lemonade. What's the matter with you?"

"Um, yeah, sure, I'd like some. Yep. Thanks." Maggie smiled vaguely at Bartholomew, who stood beside her with a pitcher in his hand.

"No problem. I *was* getting a little long-winded." He filled her glass, and seemed to get distracted himself. "Hmmm, what have we here?" He retrieved Maggie's still-full salad bowl from the far end of the long oak table, where Maggie had discarded it when she had sat down. Bartholomew pulled the pizza plate out from under Maggie's fork, set it aside, and put the salad bowl in front of her.

"Hey!"

"No salad, no more pizza."

"Wha . . . Puh . . . You can't do that!" Maggie shot the towering carpenter her mean-as-a-mad-shark look.

Bartholomew threw back his head and laughed. The roar bounced against the walls and back again. Still chuckling, he said, "Look here, young lady, every time I've come for supper in the past six months, I've watched your share of greenery go to waste. Eat."

"I don't have to! Tell him, Mom. He can't make me!"

Mara pushed her thick hair back behind her ears. "Well, I— I guess maybe he can."

"You're kidding!" Maggie's glare swept over her mother and back to Bartholomew.

His russet eyebrows lifted. "As my father used to say," he informed Maggie, "'you'll sit in that chair until you're finished.' It shouldn't take long. You'll be wanting your pizza before it cools down too much." His mild brown eyes locked on hers.

Maggie set her jaw and glared up into Bartholomew's steady gaze. This would be a cinch. Nobody, not even her mother, had ever beat her mad-shark stare.

The far-off kitchen clock ticked loudly in the ensuing silence. Seconds passed. Maggie's nose itched. Her back ached.

She ignored both, wondering if Bartholomew was made of iron and stone. He hadn't budged.

Maggie's eyes burned. She forgot how to breathe. Desperate, she pulled her when-everything-else-fails trick out of her bag. Without lowering her lashes, she crossed her eyes.

Bartholomew's mouth twitched slightly, nothing more. His eyes held steady.

It happened. Maggie couldn't do a thing about it. Her eyes blinked.

Bartholomew's mouth twitched again, but he didn't say anything, and, in the quiet dignity known only to the defeated, Maggie picked up her fork and stabbed a piece of lettuce. Head down, jaws in motion, she chewed piece after revolting piece of green stuff, her half-formed vision of being part of a happy little family dwindling as steadily as the pile of lettuce in her bowl. At last she couldn't stand it any longer.

"It's not fair! You're not even married to my mother yet. You can't boss me around like this!"

Bartholomew nodded his shaggy head as he slid onto his chair at the head of the table. "You're right, Maggie, darlin', there's nothing official until Saturday. I could have put the salad in the refrigerator until then, but I thought you'd prefer it sooner— not so soggy."

Maggie opened her mouth to retort. Nothing came out. She hunched her shoulders, lowered her head, and stabbed her fork into the last clump of dressing-soaked lettuce. She stuffed it into her mouth, swallowed, and shoved her bowl aside.

"Now may I have my pizza?" she asked stiffly.

"Sure, darlin'." The new Boss of the Universe placed Maggie's dinner plate back in front of her with a warm smile. It left her wondering how Mr. Becker could be so ornery toward someone who had the ability to make a person do something she didn't want to do and still keep her liking him.

4

Exile

MAGGIE FINISHED HER LAST bite of lumberjack pizza and glanced across the table at her mother, who looked worried about something.

"Well," Mara said, taking a deep breath, "now that you've finished eating . . ." She paused, and then said, "Honey, we have a wonderful surprise for you. Isn't this a good time to tell her, Bartholomew?"

Bartholomew's smile faded, but he nodded. "As good a time as any," he said.

Maggie's stomach lurched. "What?"

"Maggie, honey," her mother said, leaning toward her across the table, "very soon after the wedding, we're going to start renovating the house—either to live in it ourselves or to sell. Bartholomew and I are going to do most of the work, and . . ."

"No!" Maggie shouted, half-out of her chair before she even knew she had moved.

"No!" she shouted again. "We're not selling this house! I won't let you!"

"Sit down, Maggie, and hear this out," Mara said firmly. "There's something you need to understand."

Maggie scowled, but she sat, perched on the edge of her chair.

"I'm sorry, honey." Mara stretched her hand across the table toward Maggie. She couldn't reach that far, but she left her arm on the polished wooden top. "I love this house as much as you do, but . . ."

Maggie followed her mother's glance toward Bartholomew, at the head of the table.

He responded by taking Mara's outstretched hand in his right one and reaching for Maggie's with his left. He was too quick for her, catching it before Maggie could pull it out of sight.

"Maggie," he said, "it's getting harder and harder for me here in Welcome. I thought carpentry work would tide me over until my contractor's license gets approved, but Richard Becker is a powerful man in this town. People listen when he speaks. Besides blocking my contractor's license, he's turning several key people against me, so no one seems to want to hire me even to fix a medicine cabinet anymore. I have to keep driving farther and farther away from Richard's influence to find work. We might have to move somewhere completely out of his reach."

"That's stupid!" Maggie yanked her hand free from Bartholomew's and jumped back to her feet. "We can't let Mr. Becker drive us out of town—what's the matter with him!"

Bartholomew re-enveloped Maggie's flailing hand in his large one. That stopped her yelling, but it couldn't stop the tears that stung her eyes and blurred her vision. She dropped back onto her chair.

"Maggie, darlin', I can't pull it out of Richard why he wants to get rid of me. I asked him point-blank yesterday what this is all about. He didn't say a word—just clammed up and walked away."

Maggie slumped in her chair. "What chance do we have, then? Isn't there *anything* you can do?"

"If there is, I sure haven't thought of it yet, darlin'."

"Well," Mara said with a heavy sigh, "we're not going to solve any of this today. The only thing we know for sure is, we have to renovate the house, no matter what else happens." She closed her eyes for a second. When she opened them, they were on Maggie.

"Now what?" Maggie said defensively.

"Like I said, sweetheart, it's going to be quite a mess around here for a few weeks, and, well, Bartholomew and I—we've made some different arrangements for you. It's going to be a marvelous opportunity."

"That's the most suspicious-sounding . . ." Maggie grasped the edge of the table with both hands. "What opportunity? You're sending me away to an all-summer camp or something, aren't you, so you can sell the house! No way!"

"Maggie, stop that. I promise you, I will not sell the house out from under you. If we have to sell, it'll be after you return."

"Return from where? Where are you exiling me to?"

"We're not exiling you!" Mara's voice rose. She caught herself, stopped, and tried again. "Maggie, you're going to spend six weeks—a tiny, little six weeks—with Bartholomew's sister in Paris. You'll be going over alone, but returning with her in August, when she comes for her art exhibit. Don't you see— it'll be so exciting."

"I don't want exciting! I've already got camp and dancing lessons and—you can't make me go!" Maggie ran from the dining room. She raced up the stairs to her own room, slammed the door, and flung herself onto the bed, burying her face in the pillow.

What she was sure would happen next, did. There was a soft knock, and the door opened. Footsteps crossed the room to where she lay, and Maggie felt the mattress dip as her mother sat down beside her.

"Go away." The pillow muffled Maggie's words. "You're just here to try and convince me that I'll be thrilled to go to some gigantic city in a foreign country where I can't understand a thing anybody says to me."

"Maggie," Mara slowly rubbed Maggie's back, "I played the piano in a concert in Paris once. It's a lovely city. There's nothing to be afraid of. You . . ."

"I'm not afraid!" Maggie lied into her pillow.

Her mother clicked her tongue, and removed her hand, but she stayed seated beside Maggie. "Sweetheart," she said, "listen to me. If you give Paris half a chance, I know you'll love it. And you'll like Bartholomew's sister. I've talked with her on the phone. Sr. Clare is one of the nicest people I . . ."

"Sister!" Maggie jerked her head up. She'd forgotten that Bartholomew's painter-sister had become a nun.

"In other words," she wailed, "while Tanya basks in the sun at their cottage, I'll be trapped inside four walls with a bunch of flying wigglies from *Sister Act*. I can't stand it!"

"Maggie, for Pete's sake!" Mara pushed her hair back. "We've got your ticket already, and there's no backing out of that. Besides, this isn't the end of the world. It's simply a matter of your being away for six weeks while Bartholomew and I work on the house." Her tone softened. "If we wind up staying here, you and I can decorate and furnish your room together. It'll be fun. You can start dancing lessons with the fall class."

"*If* we stay. *If* Bartholomew isn't about to have to leave town, and take us with him. *If* Mr. Becker would quit bugging him." Hugging her pillow to her the way Linus would his blanket, Maggie turned over and sat up to face her mother.

"Promise me," she said, worn out by the battle. "I'll go freely into exile if you really promise—on your word of honor—that you won't sell the house while I'm gone."

"You know I won't do that to you, sweetheart." Her mother hugged Maggie, pillow and all. "Try not to worry, honey. Things will turn out okay."

Maggie nodded miserably. She wanted to trust her mother's promise not to sell Tara in her absence, but she couldn't be nearly so sure that things would work out as well as Mara wanted her to believe they would.

"Guess I'll have to pack twice," she said finally, not quite willing to let go of her pillow yet. "Once to go to the lake with Tanya, and once to go to Paris. I *do* still get to go to the lake this coming Saturday and again while you're on your honeymoon, don't I?"

"Yes, but not for as long as you'd planned. I'll need help on Friday, before the wedding, and then a couple days earlier in the second week, so we can get you ready for Paris."

Maggie sighed, and set her pillow aside. She smiled feebly at her mother. "It's okay—it's safe to leave me now. I'll be fine. A big city like Paris—it's no sweat, right?"

"That's my girl." Mara hugged her again. "I'll go down and tell Bartholomew you're okay. He's been concerned about how you'd react to the idea of staying with his sister. Come with me, and we'll play a game of Hand and Foot—just the three of us."

"What? Oh, okay. I'll come in a minute." Maggie swung her legs over the side of the bed. "First I have to call Tanya."

Mara hesitated, frowning. "Okay, honey," she said, relenting. "But don't stay on the phone too long. One of the other chefs at the restaurant is sick, and they might need me to cook tomorrow. I'm waiting for them to call and let me know."

After her mother went downstairs, Maggie walked slowly down the hall to the upstairs phone extension. How was she going to keep Tanya from laughing at her when she found out where Maggie was going to be spending six whole weeks of the summer?

"Tanya, listen. We can't get together tonight. I need to spend some time with Mom and Bartholomew before going to the lake on Saturday. And next week, I have to come home on Friday to help get ready for the wedding. Then," Maggie talked fast, "after that, I have to come home again, maybe on Thursday or so, to get ready to go to another place."

"Another place? Where? What happened that I don't know about?"

Trying to rev up enough enthusiasm to match Tanya's curiosity, Maggie said, "Thea Ronchetti is none other than Bartholomew's sister. Chew on that one for a second." Having distracted Tanya for a second, she quickly slid in her other news. "I have to go stay with her for six weeks this summer—after the wedding." Maggie braced herself for a barrage of laughter, but Tanya fooled her.

"Ooooh, you are so lucky! Dad never lets me go to Paris with him. You'll get to go to all those scrumptious stores ahead of me. I never get to do anything that neat!"

Maggie held the receiver at arm's length and stared at it. Tanya, jealous? Maggie brought the receiver back into range.

"It's okay, Tanya. Your stores are safe. I doubt if I'll have the chance to go to any of them, and I wouldn't want to, anyway."

"Oh, Maggie, Paris is lost on you! First of all, cities give you the heebie-jeebies, and, second of all, you don't like shopping! Why don't you stay at the lake with my parents, and I'll go to Paris for you?"

Maggie winced at Tanya's reminder about being scared of cities, but she didn't try to defend herself. Tanya knew as well as her mother did what being surrounded by concrete and skyscrapers did to Maggie. "I accept the switch," she said, wishing it were really possible, "as long as I get to ride Red Flash while I'm at the lake. Listen, I just thought of something. Do you still have a computer notebook you can take out there with you?"

"Sure, why?"

"Even if Thea Ronchetti—I guess I should say Sr. Clare—is stuck away in a convent, she's bound to have a computer. Maybe she'll let me use it to e-mail you. I'll give you a blow-by-blow account of life in the big city."

"Thanks a bunch." Sarcasm dripped from Tanya's words. "It's what I've always wanted—to sit at home and hear about Paris from somebody else."

Maggie didn't know what to say to that, and a long pause ensued.

"Hmmm," Tanya broke the silence. Her voice took on a calculating tone that put Maggie on edge. It was the tone her friend used for planning her wilder escapades. "E-mail conversation might be a good idea after all. Send me some nice, sedate letters that I can show my dad. I'll use them for ammunition."

"What kind of ammunition?"

"You'll see. Bye." Tanya hung up.

Maggie slowly put her own receiver back on its cradle, wondering what Tanya was up to this time.

5

Paris

BLEARY-EYED AND DISORIENTED, Maggie followed the other passengers through Customs to the baggage-claim area of Charles de Gaulle Airport, somewhere on the outskirts of Paris. The excitement of her mother's and Bartholomew's wedding, the fluttery feeling of eating cornflakes across the table from her new father, the hectic jitters of packing—it all blended into a blur of background motion as she stumbled through the airport with her knapsack on her back and carry-on case in her hand.

Six o'clock a.m. in Paris, and already the terminal teemed with throngs of people dressed in everything from saris to pinstripe suits and speaking all kinds of languages, some low and musical, some high-pitched and sharp. Maggie's heart pounded—all strangers, all in a hurry.

The crowd closed in on her. A round, chubby woman shoved Maggie out of her position in front of the luggage conveyor belt, and an equally round, short-necked man in a blue and yellow Hawaiian shirt plowed in beside the lady to haul a huge brown suitcase from the belt. Maggie couldn't squeeze out of the way fast enough, and the big case whacked against her leg. Neither of the couple apologized.

Maggie rubbed her throbbing shin. To keep from bursting into tears, she concentrated on watching the conveyor belt for her suitcase. How could her mother and Bartholomew have sent her away to this horrible, confusing place—and she hadn't even gotten to the hard part yet.

"Maggie!"

Shouted out of the crowd from fifty feet away, her name landed around Maggie like a life preserver. She turned from the conveyor belt to see the crowd part in waves, forming a path for a blue-clad bulwark of a woman—not fat or pudgy, but tall, big-boned and with a built-in aura of authority. A skinny boy about Maggie's age, with black curly hair, followed in the woman's wake.

Maggie couldn't decide which one to focus on. The nun was formidable—awesome in her size and power to command obedience from an unruly crowd of determined travelers. But it was the boy who held Maggie's attention. He was a little taller than she, and walked by leading with his left foot and using the momentum to carry his right foot and shoulder forward. His head high and proud, his eyes alert, he looked like a teenage sea captain patrolling the rocking deck of a storm-tossed ship. Maggie caught his eye, and tried to read his expression. He didn't appear friendly or hostile—merely watchful, with a touch of curiosity.

The eye-catching twosome steadily closed the distance between themselves and Maggie, until they came to a stop directly in front of her.

"Hello, Maggie; I'm Sr. Clare."

The booming Britt baritone that Maggie figured must be a family trademark drew Maggie's attention from the boy back to the nun. Even if the woman hadn't already said her name, there was no mistaking her. The navy dress and simple veil that obviously made up a nun's habit were only minor clues. The real giveaway to her identity, besides her voice, was her hair. The russet thatch of unruly locks that escaped from under the sides and front of her veil had to have come from the same genes as Bartholomew's.

"Welcome to Paris!" The big nun wrapped Maggie—knapsack, carry-on case and all—in a one hundred percent Britt hug, enveloping Maggie in a cloud of sturdy navy cotton that smelled faintly of oil paint and turpentine—the last conclusive bit of evidence that this was, indeed, Thea Ronchetti—painter and nun.

"Meet Jean-Louis Gagnon, Maggie." Sr. Clare released Maggie and drew the curly-haired boy forward. "He is our choir director's son. I thought you'd like to meet someone your own age, and he's been looking forward to meeting you."

Wishing fervently that it had been a girl instead of a boy her aunt had brought along, Maggie shook his hand stiffly, feeling the added awkwardness of the language barrier.

"I speak English." The boy's open grin and the flash of mischief in his deep brown eyes startled Maggie out of her defensive shyness.

"Me too, I speak English. Oh, yeesh!" She clapped her palm to her forehead in dismay at her ridiculous statement of the obvious.

The boy laughed too. He tried not to, Maggie could tell, but it burst out of him like a hiccup. He coughed and rubbed his hand across his mouth.

A short, awkward silence ensued, and Maggie tried desperately to think of something to say.

"Where did you learn . . ." she spluttered.

"I learned much English . . ." Jean-Louis said at the same time, with a soft accent Maggie immediately loved. He grinned, and started again. "I have learned much English in school, and also I have been learning by reading American mystery books and looking at English-speaking detective films."

Sr. Clare's hearty Britt laugh erupted into the conversation. It's room-filling magnitude startled Maggie and turned the heads of nearby travelers in their direction, but Sr. Clare didn't seem to notice the attention she had just drawn to herself.

"I can vouch for Jean-Louis' most recent learning methods," she said, still chuckling. "He doesn't stop with the mere acquisition of language skills. He practices the other skills he picks up from those books and movies, too. He thinks I don't know it, but he follows everybody who comes in or out of the church and convent, including me. If you want to know anything about anyone in our neighborhood, ask Jean-Louis."

He blushed, but flashed a mischievous smile at Maggie.

"Just like Tanya," Maggie said. "I have a friend at home who likes detective-type stuff too. Hey, there's my bag!" She leaped toward the luggage conveyor belt, but Sr. Clare moved faster. The big nun pulled the maroon case easily from the belt.

Jean-Louis took Maggie's carry-on case, and, left with only the pack on her back to worry about, Maggie followed her aunt and the French boy who spoke English and tracked people for a hobby out of the crowded terminal.

The sidewalk immediately outside the terminal teemed with more people and suitcases going in every direction. It took all of Maggie's concentration to stick with the big nun and Jean-Louis and not get jostled away from them.

Before Maggie could worry too hard about getting swallowed up in the crowd, Sr. Clare stopped at a grated window set into a stucco wall. Money and tickets exchanged hands, and the next thing Maggie knew, she had squeezed into a train car and was sitting beside her aunt and across from Jean-Louis in a set of wooden seats that faced each other.

During the train ride through the outskirts of the city, Maggie looked out the coach window in surprise. "I thought the only thing I'd see on this trip would be skyscrapers, towers and cement. It's all grass, trees and open air out there. Cool!"

"We are still far from the city," Jean-Louis said. "But inside Paris there are surprises of nature also. We have many parks, and by the river Seine there are paths on which you can walk where no cars can go. That is nice sometimes, but it is Paris itself that is exciting. You will like our city."

"Yeah, well, maybe." Recalling the noise-filled, car-jammed, nerve-jangling concrete prison of every city she'd ever visited, Maggie had trouble imagining that Paris, with its added dimension of language barrier, could be anything but the worst of them all. The closer the train roared toward its downtown destination, the harder Maggie found it to breathe.

At the train station called *Gare du Nord*, Sr. Clare ushered her out of the train, and Maggie reeled at the assault of tobacco fumes, garlic and musty newspapers that hung in the stale air of the dark tunnel. Her worst fears confirmed.

"Follow us, Maggie," her aunt urged, striding through the crowds toward the open door of another train.

Maggie obeyed. Struggling her way against, or along with, the hordes, she stuck to Sr. Clare and Jean-Louis like super glue to plastic. They poured into what turned out to be a subway car of the city *Métro* system.

Breathe in, breathe out, she told herself, falling into the same position she had held in the train from the airport—between the window and Sr. Clare, facing Jean-Louis.

Breathe in; breathe out. The fact that her feet didn't reach the metal floor when she sat down didn't help her a bit to steady herself. Trapped in the teeming mass of humanity that poured into their car, Maggie looked for something on which she could focus, to anchor herself.

At first, she only saw a blur of colors and movement, but, gradually, one face, one voice emerged from the garbled confusion surrounding her.

Singing, and accompanying himself with his guitar, an older boy of about nineteen or twenty sat on a seat facing her direction, across the aisle and several rows ahead. He had long, apple-pie blonde hair and a plain, tanned face with drooping eyelids that made him look sleepy even in the midst of his rollicking French song.

Still singing, the boy glanced in their direction. A broad grin broke out on his sleepy-eyed face, and he finished his song with a flourish of guitar chords. Scattered applause broke out among the passengers, including Sr. Clare and Jean-Louis. Maggie joined in half-heartedly. She didn't much feel like clapping for a song she hadn't understood at all.

The boy stood, took off his shabby black beret, and handed it to the man sitting across from him. Without looking back, he left his seat and strolled down the aisle in Maggie's direction. His hat followed him, passed from hand to hand. Some people dropped coins into the hat before passing it on. The boy didn't seem to notice; his eyes were on Sr. Clare.

Maggie watched, fascinated, as the tall, lanky boy approached, his guitar hanging loosely from its shoulder strap. He stopped directly in front of Sr. Clare and, shifting his guitar into place, he played and sang Maggie's aunt a gentle, lilting tune that must have also had some funny lyrics, because Sr. Clare and Jean-Louis both broke out laughing several times.

Maggie frowned. How often was she going to have to sit around feeling dumb, not understanding anything of what was going on?

The boy finished his verse with a light flicker of guitar notes and bowed to Sr. Clare, his hair falling over his eyes.

"*Merci*," she said, and pulled a battered leather coin purse from the pocket of her blue habit.

"*Non!*" Before Sr. Clare could twist the metal clasp open, the boy intercepted his hat before the passenger in the next seat could pass it to Sr. Clare.

Holding his beret closed against his guitar, the boy spoke a few words to Sr. Clare, bowed again, and walked back down the aisle. The subway train jerked to a halt, and the doors of their car slid open to spew out a flood of passengers and draw in another wave of them.

When everyone had found a seat to sit in or a strap to hang onto, and the train shot forward again, Maggie saw the beggar-musician go through the end door and into the adjacent car.

"If he's singing for money," Maggie asked her new aunt, "why didn't he let you give him any?"

Sr. Clare waved away the question with a flip of her hand. "Time to collect our things," she said. "The next stop is ours."

"I know the answer to your question," Jean-Louis broke in. "*Soeur* Clare is modest to say it. Simon is an art student in the class of *Soeur* Clare. As with many others of her students who do not have much money,"—Jean-Louis spoke quickly, before the big nun could stop him—"*Soeur* Clare helps him by giving him tubes of paint that are only used in part and other materials he needs for his study. He sings and does street painting . . ."

"Street painting?" Maggie interrupted.

"*Oui*. Many art students, and other artists too, go near the bridges of the Seine River and to Montmartre—a special area in Paris for artists and tourists—to draw and paint the portraits of people passing by. It is a good way for Simon to earn extra money for school. Plus singing—like today. But this time, for *Soeur* Clare, he sang to show that he is in gratitude for her help. She is very generous and kind to all of her students."

"Oh, Jean-Louis, I wish I were half as good as you make me out to be!" Sr. Clare rose from her seat, balancing squarely on her broad feet in the swaying car. "Simon's not a genius," she said, forgiving Jean-Louis for what she obviously considered too extravagant praise with a light swat on the shoulder, "but he has enough talent and determination to support his desire. He deserves the little help I'm able to give."

"Now," she said, "on your feet, you two. Jean-Louis, can you handle the big suitcase? I'll take the carry-on. Maggie, you hoist your backpack. We're here."

The loudspeaker crackled with a man's voice announcing the name of a stop that sounded to Maggie more like a lion's growl than a spoken word. She shook her head in disbelief. A whole six weeks of this!

The train stopped, and Sr. Clare pulled Maggie to the doors opening in the side of the car. Jean-Louis, already in motion, stepped onto the station platform ahead of them.

As soon as Maggie's feet hit the platform, a bell clanged and the subway train shot into motion behind her, leaving a gaping black hole where the train had been. Maggie's heart leaped into her throat, but she didn't have time to panic. Drawn along by Sr. Clare, she half-walked, half-ran through the *Métro* station and out into the morning crowds of Paris.

"I didn't know . . . how could there be so many . . .? Look at all these people!" No city she had ever been in before could have prepared Maggie for this madness. The panic that had darted through her in the *Métro* station grabbed her around the throat, blocking her air pipe. She struggled to breathe in spite of the deafening roar of traffic, the shouting sidewalk vendors, the racing children bumping against her. Her feet stumbled as Sr. Clare and Jean-Louis pulled her around a corner.

"Maggie? Maggie, are you all right?"

She heard Sr. Clare from a great distance, but gradually Maggie's vision cleared and her breathing slowed. She realized she had stopped walking, felt Sr. Clare's hand on her sweating forehead. It dawned on her that the frantic rumble of traffic and rush of people had dwindled to a distant hum.

Stunned, Maggie gazed around her. She stood on a thin ribbon of a sidewalk that stretched along a narrow side street with no other pedestrians in sight, and no cars either. Jean-Louis peered anxiously at her from behind Sr. Clare.

"I'm okay now." With a sheepish glance at Sr. Clare and Jean-Louis, Maggie shifted the pack on her back. "We can keep going—I'm fine. Just needed a little air." Bracing herself for another plunge into the thundering Paris battleground, Maggie took a step back toward the boulevard from which they had just escaped.

"Nope." Sr. Clare turned her around again. "That's it for the main drag. We can take these quieter streets the rest of the way home." She drew Maggie into the middle of the street and started walking down the block.

Maggie followed her and Jean-Louis, but kept looking back over her shoulder. Great—now she had a chance to get run over on a back street instead of a main one.

"Do not worry, Maggie," Jean-Louis said, catching her eye. "If a car arrives, it will travel with slow speed on this street. We will have enough time to return to the sidewalk to let it pass."

Maggie gave him a frazzled half-smile. "If you say so." She quit looking over her shoulder and tried to take in her new surroundings. "How can it be so quiet here and so crazy and wild one block away?"

"Paris has a multitude of faces," Sr. Clare belted out, reminding Maggie again of Bartholomew, "only a few of which show up in the tourist brochures."

"I will show you these faces of Paris, myself, Maggie—if my father allows me." Jean-Louis, moving along beside her with his fluid, rolling gait, threw those last words out with a surprising bitterness and pain that disappeared as quickly as it had arisen. "Will it be acceptable to you, *Soeur* Clare?" he asked in a normal tone.

"Of course. That's what I was hoping would happen." The large nun put her arm around Jean-Louis for the next several steps as they made their way down the quiet street.

Maggie wondered what difficulty with his father Jean-Louis must have, but kept silent. It wasn't the sort of thing to ask about when you've only known someone for an hour. She turned her attention back to their journey.

At the end of a couple blocks, Maggie followed Sr. Clare onto a wider street named *Rue Des Archives*, where they had to walk on the sidewalk. But not for long. Before Maggie had time to get unnerved by the rapid traffic again, Sr. Clare turned down *Rue Des Francs Bourgeois* and walked along a single short block that, on the left, was mostly taken up by a small city park. She passed the iron-gated entrance, crossed a dead end street that looked more like a long parking lot, and stopped at a wide wooden door set into a cement wall parallel to the sidewalk.

The steeple of an ancient stone church rose up from behind the wall.

"Welcome to *Notre-Dame Des Blancs-Manteaux,* Maggie—Our Lady of the White Cloaks. Your home for the next six weeks." Sr. Clare pulled the wooden door open, and Maggie stepped through the doorway into a miniature courtyard with a cobblestone pavement.

The old stone church, with its lovely stained-glass windows, formed the far side of the courtyard. Another stone building, attached to the church formed the right side. A high cement wall with a wrought-iron fence at the top formed the left-hand side of the courtyard, and a lower building than the others, plus the wall through which Maggie had just walked formed the fourth side of the little enclosure.

"It's neat. Hey!"

A little, black-uniformed Charlie-Chaplin of a man rose up out of the cobblestones directly across the courtyard from Maggie. It took her a second to realize he had run up a flight of sunken stairs that must come from the church basement or something.

Sr. Clare moved into the center of the courtyard, calling out,

"*Vous partez plus tard que d'habitude, Gérard. Est-ce que tout va bien?*"

Maggie, following hesitantly, couldn't understand Sr. Clare, but she didn't have any trouble with the first word of the little man's response.

"*Non!*" His bristle of a mustache rose and fell with the volley of words that he poured out next. His eyes darted from Sr. Clare to Maggie and Jean-Louis, and Maggie recoiled at the chill of his stare.

When the man's attention returned to Sr. Clare, Jean-Louis leaned toward Maggie and whispered.

"Gérard had to do more work last night than he wished, because of the children's group that meets once a week in the evening. He is the night watchman, and he does not like people under the age of adulthood. Now, he reminds *Soeur* Clare of an appointment they have today."

"Oh. I wonder . . . yipes!" Maggie darted aside as the night watchman abruptly ended his conversation with Sr. Clare and strode away. If Maggie hadn't moved fast enough, the little man would have run right into her. She scowled at his retreating figure, but her anger turned into a stifled giggle as she watched him storm toward the door in the courtyard wall. He not only looked like Charlie Chaplin, he walked with the identical jerky movements of the silent-movie master! When the old wooden door banged shut behind him, Maggie turned to Jean-Louis.

"I hope I don't have to see a whole lot of him while I'm here."

"Relax, Maggie," Sr. Clare said, guiding her to the right toward a set of low cement steps. At the top of the steps was another door, this one leading into the building attached to the church. "He won't be seeking you out either. Besides, he doesn't speak English, and he's usually gone by this time of the morning—except he'll be staying later when he starts coming to work on making crates for shipping my paintings overseas. Even then he'll be far too busy to pay any attention to you."

"Good." Maggie breathed easier, and followed Sr. Clare into the castle of a building that, inside, looked as though it would make a good setting for an Alfred Hitchcock movie.

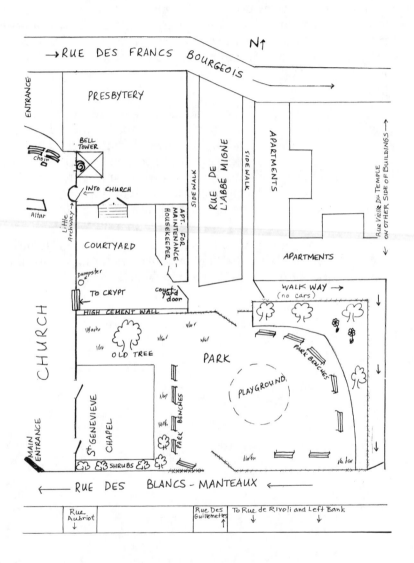

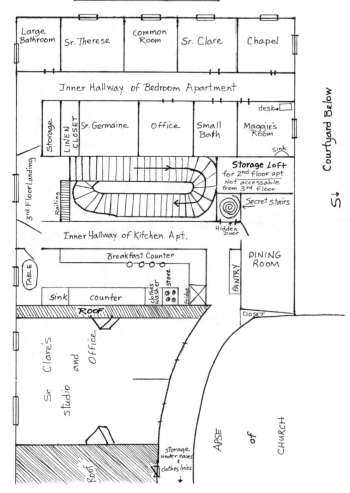

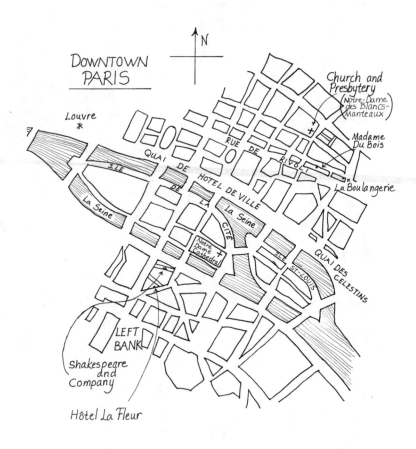

DOWNTOWN
PARIS

N

Louvre
*

Church and
Presbytery
(Notre-Dame
des Blancs-
Manteaux)

Madame
Du Bois

QUAI DE
RUE DE RIVOLI
HOTEL DE VILLE
La Seine
ILE DE
La Boulangerie
ILE
La Seine
CITE
Notre
Dame
Cathedral
ILE ST-LOUIS
QUAI DES CELESTINS

LEFT
BANK

Shakespeare
and
Company

Hôtel La Fleur

6

Beginnings

THE FIRST THINGS Maggie saw when she stepped inside the stone building were an archway on the left that looked as though it led into a church and a long, dimly-lit hall in front of her that had a winding staircase in the middle and big, medieval-type paintings hanging in a row along both sides of the hall between a bunch of closed doors. Yep, this place would make a good setting for a scary movie, all right.

"It must be a hundred feet to the ceiling," she marveled, gazing upward while following her aunt past some of the closed doors to the stairs. "Hey, why are the steps made of wood, and not stone like everything else I've seen so far? These are more worn out than my bike!"

"A stairway of this height would be too heavy made of stone," Jean-Louis said. "That is to answer one question. For the other answer . . ." Jean-Louis bent forward and ran his hand lightly over one of the concave steps. "Paris is a very old city. This is a very old building. The first monks came here over seven hundred and fifty years ago, and there have been monks or nuns walking up and down these steps ever since."

"Seven hundred and fifty years! 'Lord, love a duck!' as my Grandma McGilligan would say." Gazing upward in the middle of the damp and drafty old hall, Maggie could almost see line after line of shadowy hooded figures silently ascending and descending along the broad, circular staircase.

"Sometimes a monastery, sometimes a convent, and now only partly a convent, this building is the presbytery," Sr. Clare said. "It's attached directly to the church. We live on the top—the third floor."

"Bet there's no elevator, either," Maggie said wistfully.

Sr. Clare laughed. "Start climbing!" She shifted Maggie's carry-on bag to her left hand and held onto the handrail with her right, leading the way upward.

The higher Maggie climbed, the heavier her backpack got. These stairs would be good training for mountain biking and tap dancing, but, what about the boy coming up the stairs behind her, who probably couldn't do either of those things? She turned to look over her shoulder.

"Jean-Louis?"

A flash of defiance shot out at her when the boy realized what she was asking. "I am able to do very well, thank you."

Oops. Maggie felt her cheeks burning, and she quickly turned back around to continue her climb up into the unknown.

At the very top of the stairs, Maggie found herself on a landing at one end of the building. A small window set into the stone wall ahead of her let in a few pale rays of light, by which she could see a door to her left and one to her right.

"The chapel apartment, to your right, is a linear apartment," Sr. Clare said, "with the rooms all in a row like train cars on either side of a narrow inner hallway parallel to this central hall. That's where we have our bedrooms, office, bath and chapel.

"The left-hand apartment is set up differently, with the inner hall directly on the other side of this one, then curving off around the back of the church, which is attached to the presbytery. The rooms in that apartment are mostly on the far side of its inner hall—first the kitchen, then my studio and office, and, at the end, a little room under the eaves where we hang our laundry and store things. The dining room and pantry are at the corner of the hall, just before it curves. Got it?" A Bartholomew smile cracked the corners of Sr. Clare's mouth, and Maggie knew she was being teased.

"You'll get used to it soon enough," her aunt said seriously.

"Do the bottom two floors belong to other people?" Maggie asked, shifting the pack on her back.

"Here, unburden yourself." Sr. Clare helped Maggie shrug off her pack and set it down on the landing beside her big suitcase and carry-on case. "The second floor apartments belong to the parish priest, on one side, and his assistant, on the other. The first floor is all offices and the parish kitchen. I'm using an empty office down there to make crates for shipping my paintings to Fort Wayne for the August exhibit. They need to get there well ahead of us."

"Oh," Maggie said, stifling a sudden yawn. "Well, this sure is a big place."

"The only part of it you'll be interested in for a while is your room." Sr. Clare put her arm around Maggie's shoulders and guided her toward the right-hand apartment door. "You need a jet-lag nap."

"I will say goodbye now." Jean-Louis hadn't spoken a word since they'd arrived on the landing, and Maggie had thought he must be angry with her. But his good-bye smile was friendly. Whew, he must be the type that didn't hold onto a grudge. "I will come back this afternoon," he said, "to see if you are awake."

Maggie smiled back at him. "I'm sure I won't sleep very long. Bye." She let her aunt guide her into the apartment, and Jean-Louis put her bags inside the door before he took off down the stairs.

"He's okay—for a boy," Maggie said, not bothering to stifle another yawn.

Sr. Clare laughed and picked up Maggie's large suitcase. "It will be good for you to know someone your own age here in what must be a pretty strange place, at first."

Nice of her aunt to think of something like that, Maggie thought as she retrieved her pack and carry-on case and followed Sr. Clare down the inner apartment hall to the last room on the right.

"I'll show you around the rest of the apartment later," Sr. Clare said, putting Maggie's bag down beside an old-fashioned steam radiator that stood under a window set deep in the thick outer stone wall of a simple, wooden-floored room. All Maggie could see outside from where she stood were blue sky and the very tops of some nearby buildings.

"Come on over to the kitchen apartment when you wake up," her aunt was saying, "and I'll introduce you to the other two Sisters who live here and give you something to eat." She reached into her pocket. "Here's a set of keys. We keep the main doors of the apartments locked." Sr. Clare handed Maggie a key ring with a miniature Eiffel Tower as its ornament and two keys dangling from the ring. "It's wonderful to have you here, Maggie. Rest well, and come over to the other apartment if you need anything." She gave Maggie a hug and left, closing the door quietly behind her.

Suddenly alone in the quiet room, Maggie looked uncertainly around her. A cracked, enamel sink and medicine cabinet were attached to the wall opposite the door. The only actual furniture in the room was a little roll-top desk, a single bed and a nightstand. Pretty basic—except . . .

Maggie looked more closely at the nightstand. On the top surface sat a bowl of oranges, apples and bananas. And a wooden salad bowl with chocolates in it.

"Now, that's making good use of a salad bowl!" Maggie walked over and popped a chocolate into her mouth. "Mmm, pecans. Things are looking up. Hey, what's this?" She pulled a wide, low, rectangular metal box from the lower shelf of the nightstand and sat on the bed to examine the box's contents.

"Wow." Maggie flipped through the blank, sturdy pages of a sketchbook and the glossy pages of a paperback entitled, *Acrylics and How to Use Them*. She checked out the professional-looking palette, colorful tubes of paint and the three brushes of varying sizes all tucked neatly into the box.

"This will give me something to do besides reading the books I brought." Maggie set the box back on the lower shelf of the nightstand.

"Sr. Clare is nice," she said sleepily, snuggling under the tulip-patterned quilt on her bed.

At first, Maggie dreamt of rainbows of colors and warm sunshine, but when she awoke with a start, it was from a dream about Tara floating rapidly out of her reach and about stifling subway stations crawling with crowds of people she couldn't recognize.

She sat up sweating. The sun shone directly onto her bed from a tall window above a radiator. Where was she? Oh, yeah, she remembered with a sinking feeling—Paris. A long way from Welcome, her family, Tanya and Tara. She rose sluggishly and wandered across the room to the waist-high window. Climbing over the radiator, she settled cross-legged on the wide window ledge and looked out.

If she bent far enough over to press her forehead against the windowpane, she could see the top of the wall between the courtyard and the park next door. Past the park, across the street, there were just more concrete and stone buildings. Every evenly spaced window on what must be a bunch of apartment buildings had a miniature wrought iron balcony just big enough to hold a plant box. Red and pink geraniums made a dismal attempt at brightening the monotonous gray or beige walls of the buildings that butted up against each other like a stack of outdated encyclopedias on a shelf.

Maggie's throat tightened. Six whole weeks of concrete confinement. She turned away from the grim view and got down from the window ledge. What could she do to stop thinking about her plight? She glanced at her watch. When Bartholomew had given it to her at the airport, he had already set it on Paris time. The hour hand now pointed at one.

"Glory train! I've slept through breakfast *and* lunch!" Maggie walked over to the sink, threw some cold water on her face, and wiped it off with the soft pink towel on the wall-rack beside the sink. Ready. She strode toward the door, gearing herself up to leave the safety of her room.

With a determined twist of her wrist, she opened the door and went out into the narrow apartment hall. No one in sight. Maybe Sr. Clare and the other nuns who supposedly lived in the convent were still across the big hall in the kitchen apartment. Or maybe Sr. Clare was over there in her studio.

Maggie checked to make sure she had the keys her aunt had given her, locked the chapel-apartment door behind her, and ventured across the landing. As soon as she got the kitchen-apartment door open, she saw Sr. Clare inside, doing dishes.

"Hello, Maggie! You must be hungry." Sr. Clare reached a wet hand into the refrigerator. "I saved some Camembert cheese and part of a *baguette* for you. I've kept the vegetable soup hot, too."

Maggie sat on a stool at the brown arborite breakfast counter and munched on her cheese and a chunk of the long, thin, crusty bread her aunt retrieved from a cloth bag that looked like a stretched-out marbles holder.

"I'm afraid you'll be on your own for a couple hours this afternoon," Sr. Clare said, handing her a bowl of steaming soup. "*Soeur* Germaine has already left for the remedial class she teaches every Wednesday afternoon in the summer, and *Soeur* Thérèse went to get some office supplies from a friend of ours who saves that sort of thing for us. Your friend Gérard and I," Sr. Clare smiled teasingly at Maggie, "have an appointment that Richard Becker set up for us with someone in the shipping and receiving department at the Louvre—the art gallery. The man we're meeting will show us the best way to make the crates for my paintings. We have to get started on those as soon as possible, so I can't afford to miss this appointment. I do hate to leave you alone, but it shouldn't be for long. Jean-Louis phoned to say he'll be over as soon as he finishes running an errand for his father." Sr. Clare gathered Maggie's empty plate and bowl and put them in the sink.

"Leave the dishes," she said. "We'll do them with the supper ones. It's okay if you want to go to the park next door, but don't wander any farther until we can get you oriented, okay? I mean that, now. I don't want to have to send out a search party for you."

7

Secret Allies

MAGGIE AVOIDED Sr. Clare's eyes—not because she planned to disobey, but because she didn't want anybody to know what a chicken-heart she was in the city and that the last thought in her mind would be to venture out into the streets alone on her first day in Paris. "I won't go past the park."

"Good. We'll all be back by five-thirty for Vespers—evening prayer. Supper after. If Jean-Louis makes it over, you may see him before you see us." Sr. Clare reached for her purse at the far end of the counter. "You sure you'll be okay alone for a while? It just occurred to me—you could come with Gérard and me, if you want."

"No!" Maggie bit her lip. "I mean, I wouldn't mind going with *you,* but . . . oh, you know what I mean."

Sr. Clare smiled ruefully. "Poor Gérard. His approach to young people is a rather difficult one. Okay, see you, then."

"Sr. Clare," Maggie asked before her aunt could get away, "What happened to Jean-Louis's leg? Has it always been like it is now?"

"No." Sr. Clare stopped reluctantly. "It hasn't." She draped the purse-strap over her shoulder and smiled sadly at Maggie. "There was a car accident. I don't have time to give you all the details right now, but Jean Louis's father, *Monsieur* Gagnon, was driving him to school two years ago, when a refrigerator truck ran a red light and hit their car on the passenger side. *Monsieur*

Gagnon blames himself. He believes that if he had been more alert, the accident wouldn't have happened. His feeling of guilt is a heavy burden for him, and every time he sees Jean-Louis, he's reminded of the injury which he is convinced is his fault. So, although they used to be very close, *Monsieur* Gagnon rarely speaks with his son anymore."

Maggie gasped. "That's *terrible!* There must be something. . ."

"No, Maggie." Sr. Clare shook her head. "The best thing anyone can do for Jean-Louis right now is to refrain from interfering. I'm not even so sure he would like me telling you this much. There's the matter of his pride, you see. So, my dear, I would rather you not say anything of what you know at this point. Wait for Jean-Louis to bring it up—if he does." Sr. Clare turned briskly to the kitchen door. "I can't dawdle one more minute, or I'll miss my appointment and never find out how to make the crates. This international shipping business is still new to me. *Au revoir,* Maggie. Oh, wait, I nearly forgot."

Sr. Clare reached up and pulled a folded sheet of paper out from under the breadbasket on the top of the cupboard. "An email arrived for you about a half-hour or so ago." She handed the paper to Maggie.

"From Tanya, I bet—thanks!" Maggie hesitated. "I gave my friend your e-mail address before I left home. Is it okay if she writes sometimes? Bartholomew thought maybe you wouldn't mind."

"No problem. We'll see about your writing back soon. But right now I really have to get going. Bye again." Sr. Clare got halfway out the kitchen door this time before she swung around once more.

"I'm sorry to have to abandon you so soon, Maggie," she said with her warm Bartholomew smile, "but it won't be for long. Take an extra snack down to the park if you want. The refrigerator is at your disposal!" In a flash of blue, Sr. Clare was gone.

At least her aunt was an okay part of the city, Maggie thought as she folded the sheet of paper and stuck it into her shorts pocket. She would read it down in the courtyard or in the park.

Maggie started for the fridge, but changed her mind. Might as well start losing a few pounds right now—return home as skinny as Tanya. That would be something! She turned away from the fridge and checked to make sure she still had her new set of keys. It was going to take time to get used to this locked door business. Oh, well. Key ring in hand, she took a deep breath, opened the kitchen-apartment door, stepped outside, locked the door behind her, and stood at the top of the great, winding staircase.

"Oh, gosh, how am I going to do this?" Fighting a wild dog in the woods would be better than circling down these stairs into the unknown depths of Paris.

"This part isn't really unknown," she reminded herself, putting her key ring firmly into her shorts pocket. "I came up these very stairs this morning. So there." She started down, counting as she went.

"Ninety-seven, ninety-eight, ninety-nine. I knew there were a lot!" At the bottom, Maggie walked past the closed doors on one side and the open-doored kitchen and office on the other side. Not a soul in sight. She had the whole castle-convent to herself. At the end of the hallway, she pushed open the plank door that led outside and tried a tentative tap shuffle on the wide cement landing that formed the top of the three steps leading down into the courtyard.

"City-strange," she half-sang, half-whispered, and switched from her right to her left foot. "City-scared." Her feet couldn't come up with anything else to say, so she gave up and stood motionless, staring at the high cement wall that formed the far side of the small courtyard.

"Gregory Hines could tap this city and call it his," she said softly to the wall. "Savion danced here when he was only twelve. So, why do my legs turn to jelly when I'm faced with this much concrete? Paris, France. Oh man, oh man, oh man, what have Mom and Bartholomew gotten me into?" Maggie tried to ease her panic by familiarizing herself with her immediate surroundings.

The wrought iron fence on top of the high wall intrigued her. Weird. Was the fence to keep people out—or in? Maggie didn't want to think about it. But the gnarled little old man of a tree branch that poked through the fence from the park side of the wall was cool. That would be the first thing she'd paint with her new acrylics.

Maggie looked around some more. The next thing to paint would be the stained-glass windows in the church wall to her right.

Or the housekeeper's apartment to her left, with the wall extending from it that held the courtyard door. Three great scenes without moving a foot.

"The courtyard's okay, I guess, but it's weird too," Maggie said to herself. "Check out that sunken stairway Gérard beamed up from this morning, for instance. A place like that could hold a lot of secrets." In spite of the sweat-dripping heat of the late June sun, Maggie shivered.

She dropped down to sit on the top of the three cement steps outside the presbytery door. The radiant heat of the cement poured into her legs through her cotton shorts, making her wish for the cool, green grass of Tara, which in turn sent a wave of homesickness through her.

Maggie propped her elbows on her knees, her chin in her hands. The movement made the paper in her pocket crinkle. "Oh, yeah—Tanya's letter!" She pulled it out of her pocket and unfolded it in a rush of excitement.

"'Maggie, darling,'" she read. "Hey, this isn't from Tanya; it's from Bartholomew." Not knowing whether to be disappointed or not, Maggie read on.

> I hope you and Thea will become good friends while you're there, and that the city will not pose too big a challenge for you.
>
> Maybe you could think of the streets of Paris as a tough hill in the woods outside Welcome. You need the same kind of courage to navigate the city streets as you would to jump a ravine or leap a rain-swollen stream on a mountain bike. I know you . . .

"How could he!" Maggie tore the letter in half and shoved the ripped pieces into her pocket. Her mother had told Bartholomew that Maggie was a coward! Now he wouldn't want any more to do with her than her first father had. She sat on the step, clenching and unclenching her hands.

The door behind her creaked open, and Maggie jumped. She drew her hands across her cheeks to rub away the pain inside her and turned around to see who was there. Jean-Louis.

"I thought you were running errands for your father," she said with an edge she knew was aimed at her parents and not at the boy coming out of the presbytery. "Why were you in the convent?"

Jean-Louis's smooth seaman's gait faltered, and he stopped at the edge of the step. "My father has asked me to bring him these papers of music," he said haughtily. "I am coming from the church."

"Oh." Maggie chewed on the inside of her cheek. "I wasn't . . . I mean . . . Sorry." She held up her hands in mute apology.

Jean-Louis hesitated, but then his eyes cleared and he came to sit beside Maggie. "There is something wrong?"

"Yeah. No! Oh, I don't know. I just got a letter from my stepfather." She shrugged. "It's okay, really—I guess. Do you run errands for your dad a lot? It must be neat having a choir director for a father."

Jean-Louis' mouth tightened, and he methodically rubbed his lame leg. Realizing what he was doing, he jerked his hand away and folded his arms across his chest.

"My father," he said after a long pause, "is a very good choir director. He lives in his music. I too love music. In the old times, we would talk about it, and he wished me to become a director in his steps. I would like to have done that." Jean-Louis's face lost its momentary animation. "That is finished," he said dully. "My father has not had time for me since—since the accident that crippled my leg. I think, if he were truly to have his way, he would not talk to me at all." Jean-Louis lifted his hands in the same gesture of resignation that Maggie had used. "Enough. You received a letter from your stepfather. He likes you?"

"I—he . . . yeah, I guess so—I think. My original father didn't want anything to do with me." Maggie hadn't meant to say that. The words just popped out. She grimaced, watching Jean-Louis's eyes widen in surprise.

"He did not want anything to do with you? He was mean?"

Maggie shook her head. "He didn't have a chance to be. He died—a boating accident—a few months after I was born." She hurried on, to dispel the look of sympathy that flashed into Jean-Louis' eyes. "He never saw me, anyway. He left my mom pretty soon after they got married and she got pregnant. She says he didn't want the responsibility of a family." Maggie wrinkled her nose. "What else to say?"

Talking about Joe Sims, which she did as rarely as possible, always left Maggie feeling like a hollow log covered with moss and hidden deep in the woods where nobody would ever find it. Lost.

"But your stepfather—" Jean-Louis said, pulling her back from the void, "he does not go away?"

"Nope. Everything else, including my home that I love, may go away, but I think Bartholomew is here to stay—if he doesn't get sent off to jail, that is."

Jean-Louis's eyes widened, and Maggie rushed to explain. "Mr. Becker—my friend Tanya's dad—seems to think Bartholomew is a crook, and that he might be involved with some painting thefts that have taken place here in Paris. Can you imagine a brother of Sr. Clare being a thief? I'm dead certain he's no crook, but it would take a real Sherlock Holmes to prove it. Gee. . ." The vague beginnings of an idea slipped into Maggie's mind."

"Jean-Louis," she said hesitantly, "was Sr. Clare right? Do you really like detective-type stuff?"

"*Mais, oui*—yes." Jean-Louis's face lit up with enthusiasm. "Since my father now makes it very difficult for me to learn from him to become a music conductor, I have been thinking that perhaps I will become a detective. It is interesting to practice." He grinned and rubbed his nose self-consciously. "Sometimes *Soeur* Clare catches me in my practicing, but she does not mind, and I continue."

Maggie's heart beat lightly as hope for Tara poured into it.

"Um, Jean-Louis, do you know anything about the paintings that have been stolen here in Paris?"

"Certainly. Everyone in France knows about these."

Maggie brushed a hand across her hot, sweaty forehead. "Have you . . . um, have you ever tried to turn up any leads—you know, any clues, about the thefts?"

A grand-canyon grin emerged on Jean-Louis's face, and he nodded. "I have not tried to find clues on the paintings already stolen, but *Soeur* Clare is becoming a famous artist now. Reporters come to talk to her, and photographers take pictures of her and of the paintings she makes. I think that perhaps a thief will try to steal *her* paintings at some time—perhaps before they go to the United States. So, I follow people who come to the church and to the presbytery. I have made some very good discoveries."

"Sr. Clare's paintings? I never thought about that. It can't be that Mr. Becker thinks Bartholomew might steal *her* paintings, but, still, it's a place to start doing some detective work. Wouldn't that make for an interesting summer!" Maggie filled Jean-Louis in on all the details about Tanya's discoveries in her father's office, and especially about "SUSPICIOUS" being written across one of Bartholomew's articles.

"I know my stepfather is innocent," she finished breathlessly, "but if I can prove it, he'll get cleared in Mr. Becker's eyes, and Tara—my home—will be saved."

"Yes, we will work on this!" Jean-Louis scrambled to his feet and stood at the bottom of the steps, facing Maggie. His brown eyes shone with excitement.

"I have been following one person very much," he said, haphazardly waving his sheaf of music. "You will see the reason for this. She comes here very often, and stays long. I am suspicious that she is perhaps, to say, casing the joint. It is possible that she is a spy for the thief. So that is where we will start, no? I have read enough of the American mystery books and have watched enough films to know how to follow . . . oh!" Jean-Louis looked at the sheets of paper in his hand as though he wondered how they could have gotten there. "I must deliver these. If you like, I will return tomorrow morning, and we can detect who is coming and going from the church and the presbytery."

"Sounds great. Hey, wait a sec. Tell me something!" Maggie couldn't sit still any longer. She got up and came down the steps to stand with Jean-Louis. "Where did you find all the American mysteries you talk about? The ones you said helped you learn English? Do you get to read those kinds of books in school?"

"No, not usually." Jean-Louis looked down at Maggie from half-a-head higher than her. "Shakespeare and Company Book Shop is a wonderful place to find English books. It has many books already read by other people, so they are not expensive. I will show this place to you tomorrow, if you like. *Bonjour*." He bowed—a quick dip from the waist—and left, crossing the courtyard in his rolling gait and letting himself out through the big door in the wall.

An English bookstore in Paris! Maggie wouldn't have to be so careful about rationing the books she had brought with her. Put that together with the fact that she and Jean-Louis might find a way to get Bartholomew off the hook with Mr. Becker, and she had double good news.

Maggie sat back down on the cement steps to bask in the hot afternoon sun and in the marvelous new developments in her exile. As soon as she sat down, she caught sight of a quick movement in the far right-hand corner of the courtyard. Not the night watchman rising from under the ground this time. No, this movement was taking the form of—a cat! The small animal's orange head and green eyes peeked over the top step of the sunken stairs.

"Hello, little *chat*." Maggie felt strange speaking it out loud, but it was fun getting a chance to use one of the words she had practiced in her tourist pamphlet on the long flight over the ocean. She sat still, waiting for the cat to make its move.

Like a king in its palace, the royal feline sauntered over in Maggie's direction, pretending not to notice her but sidling ever closer toward her lap. Finally, Maggie was able to pick the teaser up. She gently stroked its back, and was rewarded with a loud, steady purr.

"Ah, so you've met *Frère* Jacques."

Maggie looked up, startled, to see Sr. Clare striding toward her from the wall door.

"Hi," Maggie said. "Is your meeting over? It wasn't very long."

"Pah! This wasn't working." Sr. Clare tapped the side of her head. "I forgot the list of dimensions I had made for the paintings I'll be shipping, which isn't so bad in itself, but I also got the time wrong. So, being an hour early, I left a frustrated Gérard at the Louvre and dashed back to get my notes and see how you're doing. It looks like you're fine, so I'll run upstairs for the canvas dimensions." Sr. Clare passed by Maggie and opened the presbytery door.

"May I e-mail my friend Tanya this afternoon?" Maggie asked, before the presbytery door could close completely behind the whirlwind nun. "I want to tell her about my trip."

"All right, but come quickly."

Maggie put a disgruntled *Frère* Jacques down and followed her aunt up the ninety-nine steps and into the left-hand apartment. They passed by the kitchen, continued down the inner hall, rounded the corner at the pantry, and turned right into what looked like a combined studio and office.

"First, my notes." Sr. Clare strode across the big room and picked up a pad of paper from a jumbled countertop attached to the far wall.

"Sr. Clare!" Maggie stopped in the doorway, awestruck. "They're beautiful! Did you paint all of them—the pictures sitting along the wall? Are they the ones for your exhibit?"

"Why, yes, Maggie. Thank you. I did. They are. Feel free to look at them when I go. Now for the computer." Maggie's aunt cleared a stack of papers away from a standard looking PC that sat in the middle of a wooden desk near the door. "You know how to work this?"

"Sure, it's just like the one I use at school."

"Hmph." Sr. Clare shook her head. "What other new-fangled things do they have in the hallowed halls of education these days? Well, I'll switch it over to the English keyboard, and, after that, you're on your own."

Sr. Clare didn't bother to sit down at her desk. She simply bent over the computer, which was already on, keyed in the change, and stepped back. "Okay, it's all yours. My address is taped to the printer here. Now, I'm off to try again, except . . ." she eyed Maggie with a wisp of a Bartholomew smile. "*Frère* Jacques stays outside. House rule."

A guilty grin betrayed the thought that had tickled the back of Maggie's mind only two seconds ago, of bringing *Frère* Jacques inside for company. Oh well. She promised not to bring the cat inside, said goodbye to her aunt, and walked over to study the paintings that leaned up against the wall in a long row.

"They're incredible," Maggie breathed.

She didn't know very much about painting, but these looked like fifteen stupendous works of art. Men and women with strong, determined, or gentle faces. Landscapes that made Maggie want to be there and soak up some of the peace emanating from the canvasses. A still life of marbles, pop bottles and a square vase of pucker-faced pansies that made Maggie laugh. She'd like to hang that one on her wall in the apartment upstairs. Her aunt must have been in some mood when she did that one!

Reluctantly, Maggie finally tore herself away from the paintings and sat down at the computer. After the first few seconds of adjusting to a new machine, she typed quickly and surely, telling Tanya all about the long plane trip during which she hadn't slept a wink, the convent that seemed more like a castle, and the wonderful surprise of finding someone her own age who spoke English.

Glancing over what she had written so far, Maggie added a line about discovering *Frère* Jacques.

"There, that should do it. Wait, two more things." She started typing again.

> *I can't believe your dad doesn't like Sr. Clare's (Thea Ronchetti's) new paintings. The ones I've just seen are out of sight—so to speak!*
>
> *Sure wish you were here too, Tanya. You would like Jean-Louis, and the three of us could have fun doing detective work together. Anyway, I have to go now. Write soon. Love, Maggie*

Maggie closed down Sr. Clare's computer and thought about what to do next. For starters, she could get an apple and a book and go back down to the courtyard with *Frère* Jacques. Or take down her new paints. Oh, rats, she had forgotten to thank her aunt for her gift. She'd have to remember the next time she saw her.

Before leaving Sr. Clare's studio-office, Maggie reached for the cover she was supposed to put on the computer, now that she was finished with it. When she picked up the beige cloth from the back top of the desk, she spotted a sheet of paper at the top of what looked like a pile of correspondence beside the computer cover.

"Oh, gosh." Mr. Becker's name, in golden script, leaped out at her. The typewritten letter underneath his heading was short, only three meager paragraphs. Maggie didn't touch the piece of paper, but she couldn't resist the temptation to read the brief communication, dated Monday, June 24, just two days ago.

> *Thea, the Board of Directors for Gallery One has decided that we need someone experienced in the field of international shipping and Customs work to handle these last weeks of getting your show together. Your brother has no experience in this realm. Therefore, we have asked him to turn his liaison work over to a member of the gallery who is familiar with these matters. In the light of that decision, we ask that, from this point on, you direct all related correspondence and questions to Kent Richards, at the Gallery One address and phone number.*
>
> *Bartholomew has done a fine job of laying the groundwork, but it is just as well he will not be involved with these last, complicated steps of preparing for the exhibit. He's too busy with married life, house renovations, work and a possible move to Ft. Wayne.*
>
> *I look forward to hearing from you either directly or through Kent Richards.*
>
> Sincerely, *Richard Becker*

"That beast! He's practically *shoved* Bartholomew out of town! Tara's as good as lost!" Maggie threw the cover over Sr. Clare's computer and charged out of the office, slamming the door behind her.

8

Trouble Brews

PROPELLED BY HER ANGER, Maggie ran blindly out of the kitchen-apartment and down the stairs to the courtyard. What right had Mr. Becker to ruin her life! She raced across the cobblestones to the wall door, threw it open, and ran to the wrought iron gate that led to the neighboring park. She yanked it ajar and raced full circle around the park twice before collapsing at last onto one of the benches that lined the edges of the park. Her anger spent, she panted in the sun-drenched heat and swiped her hand across her dripping forehead. Only then did she realize that two mothers, whose little girls had been playing in the sand lot, were staring at her and drawing the girls to themselves.

Under normal circumstances, Maggie would have blushed with shame at the discomfort she had caused. But right now she just scowled at the women, then turned her head and ignored them. Let them think she had lost her senses and become a dangerous threat to mankind. What did they know about losing everything that mattered to them and being helpless to do anything about it?

Maggie folded her arms in front of her and slumped on the bench. She felt a twinge of guilt when the two mothers herded their little girls out of the park, but was glad to find herself alone now in the island of green grass, with its sand and gravel play area. It almost felt like home here. She closed her eyes and tried not to think.

"Mademoiselle Maggie?"

Startled from a doze she hadn't known she had fallen into, Maggie opened her eyes to see a tiny rendition of Sr. Clare standing in front of her. Maggie couldn't help breaking into a grin. With her golden hair and pixie face, the little woman with the habit and slight veil that matched her sparkling blue eyes seemed more like a mischievous girl than a real adult.

"Are you Sr. Thérèse? Or maybe Sr. Germaine?"

"Oui, C'est moi—Germaine." The little nun sat down beside Maggie. *Bienvenue à Paris, et à chez nous.* Wel-come-to-here. Ah," the little nun threw up her hands, "my Hinglish!"

"Ah," Maggie threw up her hands, "my Fraanch!"

They laughed, and Sr. Germaine hugged Maggie. "It is good. Come." She got up, and Maggie, ready to be distracted from worrying about Tara, accompanied the little nun back to the courtyard.

"Soeur Clare et Soeur Therese sont ici," Sr. Germaine said, continuing through the courtyard and into the presbytery.

"Okay." Pretty sure she had gotten the drift of Sr. Germaine's simple sentence, and curious as to what the third nun in the convent would be like, Maggie ascended the ninety-nine steps and entered the kitchen apartment with Sr. Germaine.

Two blue figures, their backs to Maggie and Sr. Germaine, stood side by side, their heads bent forward into the open refrigerator.

Stifling a giggle, Maggie glanced at Sr. Germaine, who had a big grin on her pixie face.

"Bonjour, mes amis!" The little nun knocked on the wall beside her. *"Nous sommes ici."*

The two blue figures started and spun around in opposite directions—a fan opening up, then closing again as they wound up back together, facing Maggie and Sr. Germaine.

"Well, hello!" Sr. Clare said, balancing a rectangular plastic container in her hand. "We thought you must be in the park, Maggie. Were we right? Is that where Germaine found you?"

Maggie barely had time to nod, before Sr. Clare continued.

"Here is the third member of our household, Maggie—*Soeur Thérèse.*"

For the first time, Maggie looked directly at the nun beside Sr. Clare, and had to stop herself from letting her jaw drop. Before her stood the most beautiful woman Maggie had ever met. Not as tall as Sr. Clare, but a head taller than Sr. Germaine, the third member of the Convent stood regally at ease, her perfect lips parted in a welcoming smile.

"Hello, Maggie."

Even her voice was beautiful. Cultured, with the whisper of a French accent.

"It's a pleasure to meet you. Did you have an enjoyable trip?"

Maggie blinked, and got herself together enough to shake the nun's outstretched hand.

"Yes, great—it was a great trip," she stammered, and lapsed back into silence. Tanya would look just like Sr. Thérèse in about twenty years, she thought. Same black hair. Same slender elegance. She wore her blue habit like a ballroom gown. In her presence, Maggie felt as though she had just sprouted four thumbs and three arms.

Sr. Clare broke into Maggie's muddled musings. "Help us figure out what to have for supper, Maggie." She made space between herself and Sr. Thérèse in front of the fridge. "Nobody has to run off anywhere this evening, so we can take our time for a change."

Routing through the refrigerator with the two nuns put Maggie at ease with Sr. Thérèse. It's hard to stay in awe of somebody who's dipping a finger into the chocolate frosting that's trying to be pulled away from her by Sr. Germaine.

Laughing, Sr. Clare came to Sr. Germaine's aid. "That's for Maggie's welcome-to-Paris cake, you dolt!"

Maggie's first real meal in Paris—hamburgers, potato chips and the wonderful chocolate cake, "so you'd have something familiar on your first day so far away from Welcome, Indiana," Sr. Clare said—was a lot more fun than she had ever thought possible. Although they wore the same habit, all three nuns were totally different from one another—just like real people. They even knew how to laugh and joke and tease each other like real people. But, by the time dishes were done and Sr. Clare had shown her around the church, it was nine o'clock, and Maggie's head felt like it was somewhere underwater. She wasn't sorry to have Sr. Clare accompany her across the big hall to the other apartment and down the narrow inner hall to her room.

"The little bathroom beside your room is your own, and the shower works fine," Sr. Clare said. "I'll be across the hall in my room, or in the chapel for evening prayer, if you need anything. Good night." Sr. Clare hugged her. "I hope you'll come to be as glad to be here as we are to have you."

"Thank you." Maggie smiled, not at all sure about the enjoying it part, but not wanting to hurt her aunt's feelings either. "Oh, wait, I almost forgot." Maggie pulled the paint set from its shelf on her nightstand. "This is wonderful. Thank you."

"Do you like it, then? I thought it might give you something to do during the quiet times."

"Sure, it's great. Will you show me how to start? I mean—I know there's a book with it, and you're pretty busy and everything, so maybe . . ."

"Thought you'd never ask! I'll show you a few basics tomorrow, and you'll be on your way."

Maggie's hesitation dissolved, and she looked forward to learning from her aunt. But when Sr. Clare had said a final goodnight, and Maggie was left alone in her room, she put the paint box away with a sinking heart. The fun of meeting and getting to know the other two Sisters had only been a temporary distraction from Mr. Becker's letter of doom—not a full reprieve from it. Had he really managed to put on enough pressure to make Bartholomew—her father now, she reminded herself—want to leave Welcome and move to the city?

"Oh, yeah—Bartholomew." Maggie reached into her pocket for the torn halves of his e-mail. Might as well get it over with. Avoiding the awful part she'd already seen, Maggie perched on the side of her bed to read the rest of it.

> *I know you have that kind of courage, and I hope it won't be too long before you begin to enjoy Paris.*
>
> *Your mother and I miss you already, and we look forward with great anticipation to your return home. Write soon. My love to you,*
>
> *Bartholomew*

"Oh. Well. Gee." If she had only read one more line when she had first gotten the letter, she wouldn't have torn it in half. There was a P.S. from her mother, too.

Hi, sweetheart! Thinking of you being so far away is hard, but I'm hoping the time goes very quickly for you—and for us too. We're starting on the renovations tomorrow. The quicker we begin, the quicker we'll get finished.

All my love, and hugs and kisses,
Mom

Maggie carefully folded the halves of the letter together and took them over to the desk by the window. She rolled up the cover of the desk's top section and tucked the letter into one of the little slots there. Having a father who wrote you letters, and who even thought you were brave, was going to take some getting used to. Tomorrow, Maggie thought sleepily, she'd have to find some time to write home. Tonight she only had enough energy left for a shower and bed.

After her shower, Maggie felt so limp, she didn't even try to read. She just snuggled under the covers and fell asleep.

A door opening or closing somewhere in the distance woke her up, and she thought somebody must be up late, until she opened her eyes to discover the room filled with light. She checked her travel alarm.

"Ten o'clock? In the morning? I haven't slept that late since I was six and sick with the flu!"

Maggie dressed quickly, not even taking time to braid her hair, but pulling it into a Tanya-type ponytail instead. Tossing her brush onto the bed, she headed over to the kitchen apartment to see if she could scrounge up something to eat.

"Uh-oh." Halfway across the outer hall, Maggie spotted wisps of smoke curling out from under the kitchen apartment door. Three steps closer, she smelled something burning, and hesitated before unlocking the door, cracking it open, and peering into the kitchen.

"Hurry, get inside and close the door!"

Maggie did as she was told. "Yikes! What happened!"

Through the haze, she watched Sr. Thérèse quickly and efficiently pull a tray from the oven and slide some charred clumps of something from the oven to a plate. She glanced up, expressionless, when she put the plate on the breakfast counter near Maggie, but she didn't say anything.

Sr. Clare glanced over her shoulder at Maggie from where she stood at the open window, flapping smoke outward with a dishtowel. The wide sleeves of her habit flapped in rhythm with the towel.

"Oh, dear," she groaned, giving it up and collapsing onto a stool at the breakfast counter, "I was over in the chapel, and I heard you moving around in your room, so I knew you must be awake, and I ran over here to put some baguette slices under the oven broiler as a treat for your breakfast."

"Huh?"

Sr. Clare wiped her flame-red face with the towel. "Toast isn't a Parisian sort of thing," she explained wearily. "So, since we don't have a toaster, I tried to make some this way. It's tricky, because you have to watch it closely and catch it as soon as it turns brown, or else . . ." She gestured weakly toward the plate, put her elbow on the counter and her head in her hands.

"Oh." Maggie sat on a stool beside her aunt, and studied the plate's contents. Some of the chunks of charcoal still had flecks of white showing through the black.

"Gee, Sr. Clare, some of these aren't so bad." Maggie took one slightly less burned chunk, put it in her mouth, and chewed. The more she chewed, the more the charcoaled bread coagulated. She tried to push the gummy substance from her teeth without having to open her mouth, but it wouldn't budge. Her lips tightly sealed, her tongue working hard, she caught Sr. Thérèse's eye, and felt her cheeks burn.

At first the elegant nun stared back at her in unmoving silence. Then her shoulders began to shake. A mere tremor at first, the movement grew in intensity. She gracefully lifted a hand and placed it over her mouth. Too late. A splutter of laughter burst from behind her fingers.

Sr. Clare's head jerked up. "What . . ?" She looked from Sr. Thérèse to Maggie.

"Mmmpphhschmm." Maggie tried to swallow.

"Oh, Maggie, you don't have to eat that stuff!" Sr. Clare grabbed the plate and threw the rest of the charred toast into the garbage can. "If only I could learn to pay attention to what I'm doing!"

"It's an artist's dilemma," Sr. Thérèse said calmly, already recovered from her fit of laughter. "Contemplating the colors of a midmorning sky and making toast at the same time pretty much guarantee a disaster. There's no permanent damage done. Except, perhaps, to Maggie's teeth." The trace of a renewed smile fluttered across Sr. Thérèse's lips, and disappeared. "I have to catch up on the bookkeeping. See you both at lunch—which Sr. Germaine has offered to make today."

Maggie was sure she saw Sr. Thérèse's shoulders quivering again as the nun left the kitchen.

The door reopened before it fully closed behind Sr. Thérèse, and Jean-Louis appeared.

"*Bonjour.*" He sniffed. "There has been a fire?"

"Let's go down to the courtyard, and I'll tell you about it," Maggie said, ushering Jean-Louis back toward the door.

"Thank you, Maggie. Hello, Jean-Louis. Can you stay for lunch?" Sr. Clare winced at Jean-Louis's quick glance around the hazy room. "It should be safe by then."

"*Oui, Soeur Clare. Merci.*"

Maggie pulled Jean-Louis away, and they went downstairs.

"We only have about an hour before I have to set the table for lunch," Maggie said. "Sr. Clare asked me yesterday if I would mind doing that while I'm here. Not much time for starting detective work, I guess."

"But it is plenty of time to begin! Come." Jean-Louis started walking toward the courtyard door. "I will show you a place very near here that, in the future, can possibly give us some clues about the paintings that have already been stolen. Also, this place is very interesting."

Maggie dreaded heading out into the city, but the place Jean-Louis took her to was only about three blocks from the convent, and the traffic wasn't as bad as on the big main streets she had suffered through on the way from the airport the day before. She arrived at their destination still breathing normally.

"You're definitely right about the interesting part," she said, laughing, as soon as she saw what Jean-Louis said was called the

Pompidou Center, or the Beaubourg. Only a few blocks from the church and convent, the eye-catching building rose up in the middle of Paris like a collection of overgrown primary-color crayons.

"Is it for real?" Maggie scratched her head. "If I tried to tap dance the rhythm of this building, I don't know which way I'd jump first."

Hugging the entire side of the huge building, bright green spaghetti-noodle pipes competed for space with blue submarine-scope pipes that opened at the bent top and faced the sidewalk. Red box-like cars with even spaces between them stacked one on top of another all the way to the roof, and yellow pipes going sideways wove in and out among the green and blue ones. All this took place in front of a glass wall the size of which would cost a baseball team their combined life savings if they ever broke it.

"The Beaubourg contains art galleries and a library for research. The water pipes and elevators and things of that kind are located on the outside of the building so that the inside may be clear space for art. It is beautiful inside. I come often. We will return again to see the inside when there is more time—if you would like."

"Great. Any building this entertaining on the outside should definitely have neat stuff inside too!"

"Tell me of the smoke in the kitchen now," Jean-Louis said on the way back to the convent.

"Oh, yeah. Poor Sr. Clare!"

By the time Maggie explained the toast incident, and told Jean-Louis about the rotten letter from Mr. Becker, they arrived back in the courtyard, and it was time to go upstairs and set the table for lunch.

"Do not worry, Maggie," Jean-Louis said as he opened the presbytery door for her, "something will happen to help you stay in your home. And while you are in Paris, I will show you beautiful sights, and we will follow clues, in case someone is wanting to steal *Soeur* Clare's paintings. It will be fun."

"Yeah, well, maybe you're right." Maggie would never have put the words 'fun' and 'Paris' together in one sentence before, but it *was* getting pretty interesting, seeing things through Jean-Louis's eyes. His enthusiasm could be catching.

"I wonder how Sr. Clare is doing now," Maggie said, climbing the last of the ninety-nine steps and slipping her key into the lock on the kitchen-apartment door. She swung the door open a few inches and peeked inside. "All clear. Hi, Sr. Clare. Ready for us to set the table?"

"Perfect timing." The robust nun seemed to have recovered completely from her toast fiasco. She pulled silverware from a drawer in the cabinet by the sink.

"*Bonjour,* Maggie. Jean-Louis." Sr. Germaine stopped stirring something in a pot on the stove and turned to smile at them.

"Except for the two remedial reading classes she teaches, Germaine has a pretty free schedule in the summer," Sr. Clare explained to Maggie, "so she takes over most of the cooking. Thérèse is doing a basic translation of our foundress's writings from French into English and Spanish, and today it's going well, so she said she's sane enough to join us for lunch too. Which means," Sr. Clare said, handing Maggie a clump of silverware, "there are too many of us for the kitchen. You can set the table in the dining room."

"Okay." Maggie took the silverware and followed Jean-Louis and his stack of plates and bowls through the inner hall. Instead of turning right at the pantry, as she had done the day before to get to Sr. Clare's studio-office, she walked straight ahead into the dining room.

As soon as Maggie got the last spoon in place on the table, Sr. Clare and the other two nuns entered the room with the food. Everybody pulled up a chair around the rectangular oak table that reminded Maggie of the one at home, and Sr. Clare said grace.

"I hope everybody is hungry." Sr. Thérèse ladled tomato-macaroni soup into bowls.

"I got a very peculiar letter a couple days ago," Sr. Clare said, accepting her bowl of soup, "from Richard Becker."

Caught completely off guard, Maggie gasped, choking on her first spoonful of soup.

9

Detectives at Large

"CAREFUL, MAGGIE, that soup's hot," Sr. Clare said absently before continuing. "There's one thing I don't get." She cast her eyes over everybody at the table as if each one were responsible for her lack of understanding. "No, there are two things I don't get. One." She held up a sturdy, paint-stained forefinger. "If Richard Becker is so set against the way I paint now, why did he initiate the August exhibit in Ft. Wayne? I've been wondering about that all along.

"But the real cruncher is question number two. Why has he suddenly—though ever so politely and officially, of course—ditched Bartholomew as my American representative—which he's been ever since I moved to Paris—with a newcomer from the gallery? Richard says it's because of dealing with the intricacies of Customs, but, really, Bartholomew's smart enough to handle that. And to have to deal with someone I don't know at this stage . . . Can anyone explain this bizarre behavior to me—an apparently simple-minded artist?"

Maggie understood her aunt's obvious irritation, but wasn't Sr. Clare going to say anything at all about the move to Ft. Wayne? Shoot! Maggie had to work hard at paying attention to the rest of the conversation.

"If *Monsieur* Becker does not like your paintings," Jean-Louis, the budding detective, was saying, "and he has removed a person who does like your painting, then perhaps he would like the exhibit to go badly for you. Perhaps it is a way of obtaining revenge for changing your way of painting."

"Well, for Pete's sake," Sr. Clare muttered after a stunned silence, "that's an interesting theory. Is it possible? Would Richard go to that length to punish me for not painting what he likes anymore? What do *you* think, Thérèse?"

"Even if that were the case," Sr. Thérèse said thoughtfully in her lilting English, "your paintings will speak for themselves. The success of the show will rise or fall on them alone."

"Yes, of course. You're absolutely right." Sr. Clare smiled broadly. "I shouldn't try to read any more into that letter than what's there. Richard probably does just think Bartholomew is too overloaded right now to deal with a bunch of extra paperwork."

Oblivious to her cooling soup, Maggie watched in fascination as Sr. Clare continued on her new trend of thought.

"This show will be good exposure," her aunt said with what seemed to be typical Britt gusto, "and—can you believe it— Gérard, who usually gets away from here as fast as he can after work, has offered to stay late several mornings and come in on Saturdays to make the fifteen crates I need for sending the paintings. They'll need to get shipped a month, or, at the very least, three weeks ahead of the show. I'm aiming to get them on a plane July fifteenth. That doesn't give him a lot of building time, but he says he can do it."

A rapid side conversation went on in French across the table as Sr. Thérèse filled in Sr. Germaine. It ended abruptly, with both nuns smiling at Sr. Clare.

"We two are in agreement that your show will be a success, Clare. If there's anything we can do to help, give us the word."

"*Merci*, Thérèse. Germaine. With all this support, how can it be anything *but* a success? I'll give Gérard the go-ahead to start making the crates."

That was that. The conversation on Sr. Clare's exhibit was over, and, within minutes, so was lunch.

After dishes, Maggie accompanied Jean-Louis down the stairs and through the courtyard to the neighboring park, where they could talk things over. They sat side by side on a bench under the shade of a twisted, craggy-barked tree. "Sr. Thérèse speaks

English so well," Maggie said. "Did she pick it up in school and at Shakespeare and Company Bookshop too?"

"*Mais, non!*" Jean-Louis said, laughing. "She learned at University. She speaks six, perhaps seven, languages very well. She is a scholar."

"Glory! The Beauty and the Brain all in one. Shouldn't she be a professor or something? What's she doing holed up in a convent?"

Jean-Louis massaged his outstretched leg and tilted his head toward Maggie, thinking. "She is like *Soeur* Clare, I believe," he said after a while. "*Soeur* Clare is a good painter. She could make a lot of money doing only that. But she loves God and wishes to do what she feels He is asking her to do. She believes that He wishes her to share her gift to help others. So she spends much time teaching students, such as Simon. In doing this, she is happy.

"*Soeur* Thérèse is very smart and beautiful, and she could do many things, but I believe she is happy in the service of God also. This is good, no?"

Maggie shrugged. "I guess it's good. Yeah, sure, why not?" The sun's rays shining through the leaves over her head and forming a dappled pattern on her shorts and bare legs distracted her.

"Wow," she said, looking up at the twisted branches above, "I bet this tree is a zillion years old. Look how the branches loop through the iron fence on top of the courtyard wall. Which is older—the wall or the tree?"

"The wall," Jean-Louis said. "But the tree is old too. I think it is about three hundred years in age. Maggie, listen!" he said excitedly, switching to a whisper. "Look there." He pointed to the left, toward the wrought iron gate through which they had entered the park.

Maggie craned her neck to see what he could be looking at. There wasn't a single person in sight.

"Jean-Louis, what . . ."

"Shh." He put a warning hand on her arm. "Listen," he whispered. "It is the woman I have told you about. You can hear the wheels of her cart bumping on the cobblestones— because the cart is empty, I think. Continue watching."

Sure enough. Through the decorative bars of the wrought iron gate, Maggie saw the bent back of an old woman appear from the direction of the courtyard. She left their side of the street and crossed to the far side. Maggie strained to get a good look at her, but a long flowered shawl that matched and blended in with her maroon ankle-length dress hid the woman's head and shoulders from sight. She pulled a wire basket on wheels behind her.

"She must have entered the church when we were at lunch," Jean-Louis said softly. "Come, we will follow."

The next thing Maggie knew, she was being pulled to her feet and led through the park gate. She and Jean-Louis followed the old woman at a distance through the narrow back streets, Jean-Louis acting as Maggie's avid tour guide, "in the case that she turns around and sees us," he whispered.

When the old woman stopped at a vegetable stand a few blocks from the convent, Maggie and Jean-Louis ducked behind the corner *pharmacie,* and watched her purchase a bunch of carrots and some tomatoes. She stashed the vegetables in her rolling basket and plodded on down the block.

Maggie was about to tell Jean-Louis she'd had it with tailing a little old shopper and was going to suggest returning to the park, where it was cooler and there was nice, green grass, when the woman stopped again, this time in front of a cream-colored ce-ment building that looked almost exactly like all the other build-ings for blocks around. This time the old woman fumbled through her black lace purse, pulled out a key, and, cart and all, disap-peared into the building.

"*She's* the person you've been following? Why? She looks like the most innocent person in Paris."

"Do not pause here, Maggie. We must continue, in case she is watching from a window. She must not suspect we were fol-lowing her."

Maggie fell in beside Jean-Louis, but she still wanted to know what was up. "There must be a lot more interesting people to tail. Why her?"

Jean-Louis didn't falter in his rolling gait along the narrow strip of sidewalk as he led Maggie into the next quiet block, but he explained on the way. "Many times I have seen this woman at the church. She comes sometimes early in the morning, sometimes in the day, sometimes at night. She stays for a long time, sitting in church. Her head is always covered, but she is never in the same dress or shawl. I used to think it was many different women coming, but then I began to understand it was only this one."

"But, why be suspicious of an old lady with a big wardrobe? It doesn't make sense."

"Can you not see, Maggie? This woman is different from everyone else who comes to the church. She always hides under a shawl—never have I seen her face clearly—and she does not have a schedule, as the other regular visitors do. You know. One man comes at lunchtime on Thursday. Another woman comes each morning before she goes to her job of housecleaning. Two women who are sisters come on Wednesday, on their way to get ice cream at St. Michel. But this woman, she is not like them."

"Well, okay, that's interesting—a little bit—I guess."

"Wait, there is more." Jean-Louis hardly slowed his pace as he led Maggie down a block lined with all kinds of meat and fish and flower shops. "When this woman leaves the church, she always starts away in a different direction. But," Jean-Louis paused for effect, "she always ends at the same place, the apartment building. Why do you believe she does that?"

"I don't know!" Maggie said, laughing. She took her eyes off the beautiful roses set in buckets in front of the flower shop to face Jean-Louis. "You've convinced me. She's interesting enough to practice on. Maybe *she's* planning to make off with Sr. Clare's paintings!"

"*Oui*. She will disguise them as groceries in her cart! Let us begin—Sherlock Holmes and Miss Marple. Together we will solve all the crimes of Paris!"

Yes!" Maggie slapped Jean-Louis's upraised palm. "All painting thieves of France, sit up and take notice. You haven't got a chance!"

"*Bon,* it is settled. So, now we will tour. You will come to know—and to love—my home of Paris." Jean-Louis led Maggie through a postage-sized park set between an inviting *patisserie* and a sidewalk café. Bob-necked pigeons waddled near their feet, pecking at crumbs dropped by people who sat on the three or four wrought iron benches eating pastries.

"First," Jean-Louis said, you must see the Seine River, Notre Dame Cathedral, and the Left Bank. The Left Bank is where famous writers used to come. They still do. It is where Shakespeare and Company Bookshop is."

He led Maggie from the relative quiet of the back streets into the nerve-jangling city center. "Here, we cross *Rue de Rivoli,* a major street of Paris."

Maggie's heart hammered in her chest as she ran with him across the wide, traffic-choked street. Happy to find herself still alive on the other side of the gauntlet, she stuck close to Jean-Louis as they approached a bridge that spanned the famous Seine River.

"Notre Dame Cathedral is on an island called *Ile de la Cité,*" Jean-Louis said. "We will cross this bridge to the corner of *Ile St. Louis,* and, immediately after that, a second bridge to *Ile de la Cité,* which is called that, because it is where the city of Paris began."

"Cool. Hey, look at the boat! A double-decker! There must be a hundred people on it. That's got to mean it's a tour boat. Let's take a ride on one of those! Could we?"

"Yes, if you want. But not in the day. I will take you sometime in the evening. Paris by night is best for *Les Bateaux Mouches,* the tour boats. Then we will see Paris, the City of Light. The *Tour Eiffel,* the Eiffel Tower, is at its most magnificent at night, and many other places too."

"Okay, I'll wait for that. Here's our other bridge already."

They crossed over the second expanse of water and around to the front of an immense stone church with twin spires stretching into the sky. Between the spires, in the middle of the high front wall, there was a huge stained-glass window shaped like a geometric flower.

"Good grief! They don't come like this in Welcome, Indiana! It's fantastic. What is it?"

"This," Jean-Louis said, the pride obvious in his voice, "is Notre Dame Cathedral. You know of *The Hunchback of Notre Dame,* probably. Do you like our Cathedral?"

"Like it?" Maggie breathed. "It's stupendous! I never knew a church could look like that. I mean—I've seen pictures of it, I think. It kind of looks familiar, but . . . wow! I can't believe a church this big is on an island." Turning to see if she could locate signs of water on every side, Maggie glanced behind her. She didn't see any water, but what she did see startled her.

"Oh, gosh, look!" She grabbed Jean-Louis's arm and pointed to the other side of the street.

There, on what Jean-Louis had called the Square, lots of artists sat on folding chairs behind easels or on the grass with sketchpads in their laps. People wandered around among them, looking at their work, and before some, a person stood or sat, getting their portrait painted or sketched.

"What is it, Maggie? Such artists are always at work in these areas. Oh, it is Simon! Shall we go say hello to him?"

Maggie hesitated. She hadn't liked Simon much on the train. But, oh, what the heck, why not? "Okay, let's go. It's kind of neat running into someone I recognize." She walked with Jean-Louis over to where Simon sat on the grass, a large drawing pad in his lap. His long, straight hair fell forward over his shoulders as he sketched.

"*Bonjour,* Simon." Jean-Louis held out his hand to the lanky art student. "I would like you to meet Maggie, the niece of *Soeur* Clare. May we see what you are sketching?"

"Hey, Jean-Louis, how are you?" Simon switched a piece of charcoal to his left hand and shook hands with his right. "Hello, Maggie. I remember seeing you on the train yesterday."

Maggie stared. "You speak English!"

"Of course—I'm American." He laughed—not such a bad laugh, Maggie decided. "I've been in Paris for almost four years, so I probably look like part of the original landscape by now."

"*Mais, non!*" Jean-Louis shook his head fervently. "That would take perhaps another one hundred years. But, the drawing you are making is part of the landscape for a very long time. You have done something nice with Notre Dame. It is a good background. And the old person in front . . ." Jean-Louis's breath caught, and he looked closer. "Maggie, you must see!" His dark eyes glowing, he pulled Maggie to where she, too, could see over Simon's shoulder.

"Well, I'll be flabbergasted and amazed!" Maggie hit the side of her head with her palm. "It's her, isn't it? Our little old shopping lady and her cart. So that's what she looks like. She looks so frail and old without her shawl, Jean-Louis."

Simon looked quizzically at Maggie, then at Jean-Louis. "So, who is she? She comes past here sometimes when I'm sketching, and she's perfect for this piece. Old church—old woman. Get it?"

"Sure. Neat. That's great, Simon." Forgetting about the identity of the old woman for a second, Maggie looked at the sketch simply as a drawing. "I really like it. I like the way you've done the church—the way it's so hazy in the background, but strong. I almost didn't see it at first, but there it is—protecting the lady. It's like nothing can hurt her, as long as it's back there, sheltering her." Maggie looked up, caught the gangly artist's eye, and stuttered, uncertain. "Oh, well, you know, it's just how it makes me feel. I don't know much about art, really . . . ." Maggie broke off. Why was Simon looking at her like that? Maybe she shouldn't have said anything about his picture. Maybe she had insulted him somehow. Made him angry.

"Here." In a swift, sure motion, Simon ripped the page from his pad. "It's yours."

"Oh, no!" Maggie put her hands behind her back. "I didn't mean for you to . . ."

"Take it," Simon insisted, rolling up the sketch and securing it with a rubber band. "You're the first person I've ever met who has understood exactly how I felt about a piece of work I've done. I want you to have it. When I'm old and famous, you can sell it and make your fortune."

"Never! I won't ever sell it. It'll be a wonderful memory of Paris that I'll keep always. Thanks, Simon." Maggie accepted the rolled up sketch gingerly, not wanting to bend or crush it in any way.

Jean-Louis, who had been quiet while Maggie and Simon had conducted their transaction, now spoke up. "Simon," he said seriously, "you said that this woman in your picture comes by sometimes when you are working. Is it always here, by the church, that you see her?"

"Not always," Simon said, rubbing the back of his neck while he thought it over. "Sometimes I see her here by the Cathedral, sometimes over on the Left Bank. Why?"

"We—Maggie and I—need to know more about her. Where does she go? Does she meet anyone? What does she do? Will you tell us if you see her again and notice any of these things?"

Simon looked skeptical. "You two aren't up to mischief, are you?"

"Oh, no, it is nothing like that." Jean-Louis looked at Maggie.

Her mind still on the first real piece of artwork she had ever possessed, Maggie nodded distractedly. "Nope, no mischief." Out of the corner of her eye, she saw Simon grin.

"It is possible that knowing about this woman will help *Soeur* Clare," Jean-Louis went on. "If we can be sure nobody steals her paintings before she sends them away for her exhibit, that will be a very good thing."

"I see. Well, if it can help keep Sr. Clare's paintings from getting stolen," Simon said, pulling a fresh piece of charcoal from a little box beside him on the grass, "I'll do what I can. Come back around tomorrow or the next day, and maybe I'll have another sketch of the poor old woman and her activities for you. Meanwhile, be sure nobody steals that sketch from you, Maggie!" He dismissed them with a chuckle and went back to work, starting a new sketch.

"What now, Jean-Louis?" Maggie asked, as they left the Square and returned to the sidewalk.

"It is very fortunate to run into Simon," Jean-Louis said excitedly. "On our first day of detecting together, we have discovered a very important piece of evidence about our suspect." He directed Maggie toward the opposite side of the island from which they had come. "Immediately past the statue of Charlemagne on his horse, there is the bridge that leads us to the Left Bank. I will show you Shakespeare and Company Bookstore."

"Great. I want to see this place that perfected your English."

Halfway across the wide cement bridge, Maggie, toying with the rubber band Simon had put around her sketch, stopped and turned to face her new friend.

"I just thought of something, Jean-Louis. Are there any art galleries in this area? Does Sr. Clare have any paintings in them?"

"There are many galleries," Jean-Louis said, leaning with his back against the bridge railing. "*Soeur* Clare has one painting in a gallery very near to here. I was meaning to take you there as a Paris surprise for you. This one is what made me interested in watching to see that her paintings do not get stolen before her exhibit."

"How did it do that? What does one of Sr. Clare's paintings in a gallery near here have to do with the possibility of her other ones getting stolen?"

"A Dumolin painting, the last one known to have been stolen, was on its way to the gallery that has the one by *Soeur* Clare in it."

Maggie whistled softly, and came to lean forward over the railing, watching another two-story tourist boat float past them under the bridge and on down the river. "So, you think the one she has in the gallery might get stolen?"

"Not that one." Jean-Louis swung around to look out over the river too. "All of the paintings that have been stolen in the past three years have been taken before they reached the gallery to which they have been going. How and to where they disappear, nobody knows. Every person in Paris is suspect!"

Maggie wrinkled her nose. "That doesn't narrow it down much, does it?"

"*Mais, non.* But, do not worry, Maggie. We can do it. The doctors said I would never walk without the aid of crutches, and—*voila!*" He stood straight, his arms stretched aloft, and Maggie applauded enthusiastically.

Jean-Louis bowed, and began walking again toward the far side of the bridge. "We continue to Sr. Clare's gallery and Shakespeare and Company Bookshop."

Musée Millénaire Nouveau was a small gallery on the West Bank that Maggie liked immediately. It had only one main room, with nooks and crannies branching out from it like wheel spokes. It didn't take her long to locate the spoke that contained her aunt's painting.

"It's the same style as the ones I saw in her studio yesterday. The lines are so clean and strong. Powerful, like. Who's the fellow in this one, Jean-Louis? He's a man after my own heart— surrounded by countryside, animals and birds."

"He is St. Francis of Assisi," Jean-Louis said. His expression told Maggie he was surprised she didn't know, but he didn't laugh at her. "He is from Italy, and he lived at around the same time that the church where you are staying was built. There are many stories about his love of animals and how they obeyed him."

"No kidding? If he's that famous, then maybe I'll find a book at your English shop that has those stories in it. Let's go!"

The wonderfully jumbled, old-world flavor of Shakespeare and Company Bookshop captured Maggie's heart instantly. Its weathered two-by-four bookstands outside the front door overflowed with pile after inviting pile of mostly second-hand books.

The wooden front of the book-crammed building automatically set it in another world from the cement, stone and wrought iron that dominated most of the other buildings Maggie had seen so far in the city.

Wandering inside through the open door, she feasted her eyes on floor-to-ceiling bookshelves sagging under the weight of what must be thousands of books. She scooted carefully around other book-browsers in the narrow aisles between the shelves. It was going to be real easy to spend lots of time in this musty, dusty treasure chest of English-speaking books too many to count. She didn't spot any books about St. Francis, but she could look another time.

"We should go there at least once a week," Maggie said on the way home.

"We can go often," he agreed, swinging along beside her with his sea-captain walk. "But there are other places in Paris that you will also enjoy. You will see."

Maggie merely grinned. Maybe Jean-Louis was right, but even if there was hardly another thing she would like in this strange and forbidding city, she knew she would always find a refuge at Shakespeare and Company.

Still in a happy daze when she opened the door in the wall to the church courtyard, Maggie moved too slowly to avoid the ensuing collision.

⊷⊷❧ **10** ❧⊷⊶

The Dripping Umbrella

"YIPES!" THE IMPACT of the blue hurricane shot her backward into Jean-Louis. He stumbled, but regained his balance, holding himself and Maggie upright.

"Ah, there you are! Sorry, Maggie. Are you all right? What's this—a souvenir?" Sr. Clare picked up the rolled sketch that had flown out of Maggie's hand in the collision and returned it to her. "Hello, Jean-Louis." She grinned sheepishly as she straightened her veil. "I'm hurrying to pick up a few things for supper." She started out the wall door, but caught herself.

"Almost forgot," she said, turning back around. "Your mother called, Jean-Louis. You have company coming for supper, and she wants you home to help get ready. And Maggie, you got an e-mail from your friend Tanya. It's still unopened—the computer's on. See you."

"Wait! Is it okay if I write Tanya back when I read her letter?"

"Of course. Then shut down the computer, would you? Bye." Sr. Clare flew out of the courtyard door, and Maggie had visions of her colliding with a few other people by the time she got to the grocery store, or wherever a person bought regular groceries over here. She turned to Jean-Louis.

"Can you stay long enough to see what my friend's letter says?" Maggie shifted her shoulders and shook her legs to make sure all her bones were still in their right places. "The sketch is okay," she said, examining the roll. "Thanks for being such a

76

good backboard. I would have gone flying all the way back to the Left Bank!"

Jean-Louis laughed. "I am happy to be of service. But, no, I must go. My mother gets very anxious when she fixes food for guests. I will come tomorrow morning. Like my father, I get up early usually. Do you? If you do, we can begin right away our work of—as you say—tailing suspects."

"Name the hour, and I'll meet you here in the courtyard."

"Six-thirty?"

"Done. I usually get up early at home, too, for a bike ride."

Jean-Louis left, and Maggie walked across the courtyard toward the presbytery steps. As soon as she reached them, the outer wall door from the street slapped open behind her, and she turned to see if Jean-Louis had come back for something. At first, nobody appeared in the open doorway, but then Gérard bustled into the courtyard with a pile of boards in his arms. He kicked the door closed behind him, and one of the boards slipped out of his grasp.

Maggie put her sketch to the side on the bottom presbytery step and ran over to help. "I can carry this inside for you," she said, reaching for the loose board.

Non! The little night watchman shook his head vehemently, and dumped the rest of his boards on top of the fallen one. With sharp words and a jerk of his head, he marched across the cobblestones and into the presbytery.

Maggie looked down at the pile of lumber, shrugged, and went back to the steps for her sketch. Luckily, she got it in her hand before Gérard charged back outside, pulling a flatbed wooden wagon. It bounced wildly behind him on the steps and bumped across the courtyard. In swift, ferocious movements, Gérard loaded the wood on the wagon and yanked it around again toward the presbytery. Maggie ran inside ahead of him.

"Grouch," she muttered, storming up the steps. "If he's that down on kids, he deserves never to get any help."

Maggie fussed and fumed her way upward, but by the time she reached the kitchen apartment at the top, she forgot about everything except the fact that she had received an e-mail from Tanya.

"Anybody home?" Maggie called, unlocking and opening the kitchen apartment door. No response, so she went straight to her aunt's office. "I wonder how Tanya's doing at the lake."

Focused on what her friend would have to say, Maggie didn't spend time looking at any of the paintings propped against the outer wall in Sr. Clare's studio-office, but sat down right away in her aunt's rolling chair, clicked onto Tanya's letter, and read:

> *Guess what I found in my dad's den here at the lake. On his desk calendar, he's underlined Monday, July 16, and beside the date he's scribbled a note saying 'Return with Ronchetti paintings.' That means he's going to Paris. And it means my mission for the next two weeks is going to be to get him to take me with him. Stay tuned!*
>
> *Your friend, Jean-Louis, sounds great. But I can't show my dad your letter—not with that stuff about him and Thea Ronchetti in it. Or the part about doing detective work. He thinks I sneak around too much as it is. Send some of those sedate, responsible e-mails I told you about—and hurry! That will be my best ammunition for convincing him to take me along.*
>
> > *See you soon. Cross your fingers!*
> > *Tanya*

"Rats!" Maggie printed Tanya's letter before deleting it and typing out a reply.

> *Dear Tanya,*
>
> *If your dad is only coming to go back home with Sr. Clare's paintings, and if he brings you, it means you'll only be here for a couple days at the most. That's way too short a visit. Can't you get your dad to let you come over earlier, and go home with him?*
>
> > *Love, Maggie.*
>
> *P.S. A sedate and respectable letter to show your dad will be right behind this one.*

Maggie sent that note into the 'outbox' and banged out a letter that would lead anybody to think all she did in Paris was sit in the park and use her new acrylics to paint dainty pictures of children playing in the sand box.

"That should do it," she said, sending both letters on their way, and closing down Sr. Clare's computer. Sketch and letter in hand, she left her aunt's office. As she approached the kitchen, she heard the light clanking of pots and pans. Somebody, probably Sr. Germaine, must be making supper.

That cheered Maggie up, if only a little. The afternoon's tracking and touring had given her an appetite that all her uncertainty about the future couldn't diminish.

"Hi, Sr. Germaine." She poked her head into the kitchen. "Mmm, spaghetti?"

Sr. Germaine returned her smile. *"Bonjour,* Maggie. *Oui,* spaghetti."

"I'll put this stuff over in my room and come back and help, okay?" Maggie waved her scroll and letter and pointed toward the opposite apartment.

Sr. Germaine nodded. *"Bon,* Maggie. Help is good."

Maggie crossed the hall with rising spirits. Maybe Tanya really could come early. That would be terrific.

Ten minutes later, back in the kitchen, Maggie worked harder at communicating with the little golden nun than she did on the meal. Sr. Germaine's English was almost as limited as Maggie's French, but by suppertime Maggie knew how to ask for bread at the bakery in French, and Sr. Germaine grew adept at "Gimme five!" and "Catch ya later."

By the time Maggie got to her room in the evening, she was glad to stay put there and catch up with what was happening to Scout and Jem in *To Kill a Mockingbird,* which she had started on the plane and hadn't had a chance to look at since.

She read a lot later than she had planned to, but she still managed to make it to the courtyard at six-thirty the next morning.

No Jean-Louis yet, but he would be there soon. She put Tanya's letter in her shorts pocket and sat on the presbytery steps to bask in the not-yet-hot early morning sunshine and wait.

The wall door opened, and Maggie got up expectantly.

"Oh! Hi, Sr. Clare. Hey, Jean-Louis."

Sr. Clare zeroed in on Maggie. "Ah, good, another early riser. Good morning, Maggie." Her aunt hugged her and kept talking at the same time. "Tomorrow, *you* can go for the breakfast *ba-*

guette." She hoisted the long, thin loaf of bread like a trophy. "This morning, after breakfast, the three of us can move the books to the new library shelves in the dining room. We should be able to polish the job off by lunch. That'll give us plenty of time this afternoon to take a loaf of Sr. Germaine's fresh Italian bread to Madame DuBois. She's an elderly shut-in—Gérard's aunt. We visit her regularly on Germaine's baking day, and on Sunday afternoon."

Maggie exchanged grimaces with Jean-Louis. A whole day lost.

Seemingly unaware of any adverse reactions to her plans for them, Sr. Clare ushered Maggie and Jean-Louis into the cavernous hall and up the ninety-nine steps to the landing at the top. "Do you both good to perform an act of mercy," she said, unlocking the kitchen-apartment door, "and put something else into your young heads besides running the streets and touring the hotdog stands." She winked at Maggie.

Hoping Sr. Clare hadn't really meant that about going by herself to get a *baguette* the next day, Maggie managed only a feeble smile for her aunt.

By eleven o'clock, when she and Jean-Louis had dismantled the old makeshift shelves in the hall near the pantry and had finished hauling books to the new dining room shelves, Maggie was hot, sweaty, grumpy and hungry. The aroma of baking bread that emanated from the kitchen was driving her crazy.

"I'm starved," she muttered to Jean-Louis a half-hour later, "but at this rate, we'll be too tired to eat." She puffed down the stairs with her end of the last cracked plank. "And we'll never get back to our detective work."

Jean-Louis swung down the last step with the front end of the board. "We are not getting to the bottom of any mysteries, but we are getting to the bottom of these steps many times."

"Not funny." Maggie opened the presbytery door with her free hand. "It's starting to rain too. Yuk!" She and Jean-Louis lumbered across the courtyard to the dumpster beside the crypt steps, dropped their board, and raced back to the presbytery. Jean-Louis won, but Maggie leaped inside only half a step behind.

"One job done," she said. "Just in time to get cleaned up for soup and cheese."

After lunch, Maggie barely caught her breath before finding herself trooping along beside Jean-Louis and behind Sr. Clare again, this time under an umbrella and with a basket of bread wrapped in a plastic bag under her arm. Oh, well, it wasn't a good day for touring or detective work anyway, and it felt good to be getting used to at least this small neighborhood section of the great stone and wrought iron city. She twirled her umbrella in one hand. "I feel like I'm in the middle of two Gene Kelly movies, *An American in Paris* and *Singing in the Rain.*"

"Look at what building we are approaching," Jean-Louis said softly.

Maggie stopped twirling her umbrella, and looked. At first, she didn't see anything distinctive about the flat-fronted beige building Sr. Clare was walking toward. Then it hit her. "The shopping-cart lady!" she whispered.

"Oui." Jean-Louis betrayed his excitement by stumbling over the single step leading into the apartment foyer. Until now, Maggie had never once seen him trip over anything. "This is most fortunate," he whispered over his shoulder. "Keep watch carefully."

Sr. Clare buzzed a fourth-floor number, got an answering buzz, and pulled the door open that led into the main body of the building. Entering a musty hallway that reminded Maggie of the empty kind of feeling the Roxy had back home, the nun walked straight toward a brass-trimmed elevator that had to be at least a hundred years old.

Close behind her aunt, Maggie held her breath against the moldy odor of stale air and, like Jean-Louis, checked the dimly lit hall for the hint of an old lady with a shopping cart. Neither a shadow of her nor a ghost of anyone else appeared before they all crowded into the elevator and ascended to the fourth floor.

The tarnished gilt doors opened to an empty hallway identical to the one on the first floor, and Sr. Clare went to knock on the door directly across from the elevator. Without waiting for a response, and moving in what seemed a well-formed habit, she slid a key into the lock, opened the door, and entered a cramped room as dark and dingy as the hallway.

A cold-fingered loneliness seeped into Maggie's bones, the kind of feeling she knew she'd get if she had to leave Tara. She stared into the dark bleakness of the apartment, searching for signs of life.

"Qu'est-ce que tu veux?" The voice croaked out of the depths of a davenport ahead of and to the right of Maggie. It took a couple seconds to pick out the vague form of an old woman wrapped in the folds of a blanket of some sort. Maggie shuddered. Why was the lady lying here in the dark like this?

"C'est moi, Madame Dubois." Sr. Clare spoke more gently than Maggie had known a woman of her size and energy could, but the enshrouded form of Madame DuBois only spewed back harsh, guttural scratches. She jabbed a bony finger toward Maggie and Jean-Louis.

Sr. Clare shook her head, and, still speaking calmly in French, she picked up an empty basket from some sort of end table and replaced the basket with the full one Maggie had brought. She handed Maggie the empty basket and moved to the window beside the divan. She started to pull the drapes open, but Madame DuBois recoiled deeper into the shell of her covers and screeched,

"Non! Ne touchez pas ces rideaux! Je deteste la lumière!"

"She says she hates light," Jean-Louis whispered quickly into Maggie's ear.

Sr. Clare clicked her tongue, but she moved away from the window.

Maggie's eyes had grown accustomed to the dark now, and she saw Madame DuBois, in her agitation, lose her grip on her crocheted afghan. The afghan slipped sideways, and before the old woman could yank it back into place, Maggie caught a glimpse of her face—the face in Simon's sketch. The old imposter!

Maggie could hardly wait for Sr. Clare to take leave of the phony invalid and her oppressively dark and musty apartment. Inches behind her aunt as the nun opened the apartment door, Maggie almost missed Jean-Louis' slight nudge from behind and the tilt of his head toward the apartment corner next to the door.

There in the corner stood a rack that held a long black coat layered with dust. Behind that, on the bare wooden floor, a pool of water shimmered in the weak beam of light that came into the room from the hallway. The source of the water was a dripping umbrella propped up against the wall behind the long coat.

Nauseous with bottled-up agitation and closed-in mustiness, Maggie jittered her way down the elevator and out of the apartment building. She gulped in the fresh air and held up her face to catch the intermittent raindrops that still fell from the gray sky.

Last in their single-file line on the narrow sidewalk, Maggie walked as close as she dared to Jean-Louis' heels, her head tilted forward to hear the conversation between him and Sr. Clare. She jumped when a silver Renault passed them from behind, two wheels on the sidewalk. It wasn't going fast, but still . . . that was one Paris custom Maggie might never get used to. How did Jean-Louis and Sr. Clare do it? Neither of them seemed to notice that the car grazed their elbows. It took Maggie a second to realize that Jean-Louis was busy pumping Sr. Clare.

"For how long has Madame DuBois been unable to go out of doors?" Jean-Louis was asking.

"Well, let's see," Sr. Clare said as casually as if she were sitting in the convent kitchen. She tapped the sidewalk with the metal tip of her closed umbrella—counting as she walked. "Gérard came to us a good six to eight months ago, I'd say, to tell us his aunt had had a stroke and was confined to her apartment. He asked if we would visit her, which we did, and have been doing every baking day and Sunday since."

Sr. Clare's words sent a shiver down Maggie's back. Was their practice suspect for real? Were Sr. Clare's paintings really in jeopardy?

"Madame DuBois *must* be up to something!" Maggie said as soon as they got home to the courtyard and Sr. Clare left them to go inside. "Otherwise, why would the old phony try to fool Gérard and everybody else into thinking she can't walk?"

"From now on, we will watch her especially closely." Jean-Louis led the way to the presbytery steps to sit down. "I do not think she realized that we recognized her. You did very well not to react when the blanket fell from her face, Maggie."

Maggie blushed. "Aw, thanks, Sherlock. You did great too. But, listen—with only two weeks to go before Sr. Clare's paintings get shipped, we'll have to step up our detective work. If she doesn't do us in herself by nabbing us to work every day."

"Ah, *oui*. My father, too." Jean-Louis shifted on the step and stretched his injured leg out straight, his heel resting on the cobblestone pavement. "He will not talk with me in other ways, but he often asks of me to come here or to other places in the city for music or things he needs."

Maggie could hardly bear to look at the pain in Jean-Louis' eyes as he talked about his father's rejection of him. But, as Maggie was discovering, his pain often fell away as quickly as it appeared, the way it did now.

"Many time," Jean-Louis said, brightening, "I do not mind these errands, for I meet many musicians and singers. It is very interesting, and . . ."

The door behind them opened, and Jean-Louis broke off.

"*Bonjour,* Maggie. *Bonjour,* Jean-Louis." Sr. Germaine, her golden hair sparkling in the sunlight that had replaced the rain, stepped out of the presbytery and bounced down the three cement steps.

"*Pour vous,* Maggie, *de Soeur* Clare." She handed Maggie a sheet of paper. "Catch ya later." With a wave to them both, she crossed the courtyard and left through the wall door.

"Catch ya later?" Jean-Louis eyed Maggie accusingly.

"I'm a good English teacher, no?" Maggie grinned in wide-eyed innocence. "What is it she gave me, anyway?" Maggie glanced at the paper Sr. Germaine had handed her.

"Oh, gosh—another e-mail from Tanya. It says it was sent at fifteen-hundred hours. That's three o'clock, right? Hey, it must have just come! I hope, I hope, I hope she can come. And especially, I hope she can come earlier, ahead of her dad."

"Read, Maggie; and you will see," Jean-Louis urged.

"Oh, yeah, okay." Maggie cleared her throat. She read:

> *Guess what! I can't come early, like you asked in your letter, but Dad said I CAN come with him! I didn't have to wheedle him into it, or anything. He offered! Can you believe it!? We'll be staying at Hôtel La Fleur. Dad said it's somewhere in an area called the Left Bank. Is that far from where you are? The only hitch is, he wants the time together—just him and me (!!!). He says we're always at each other but never with each other. (That'll be interesting.) He also said it'll be a big holiday then and we'll be too*

busy to see you on Saturday, when we get there. I
think he's afraid to let me out of his sight for one minute!

There's a famous fashion designer who lives in
Paris—Jacques Brière, in case you've heard of him—
who's a friend of Dad's, and he's invited us to come for
dinner and to watch the big fireworks with him the
night of our arrival. We'll have to sleep off jet lag
when we get to the hotel. I think Dad's planning for
us to see you on Sunday.

"Fireworks?" Maggie asked, looking up at Jean-Louis. "Wait,
never mind. I'll finish reading, then ask you." Maggie continued:

Here at the lake, Dad's back and forth, like always,
and Mom and I will go home on July 10 so I can get
packed and ready for—ta da—Paris! See you soon!!!
Write and let me know about the weather there and
what people wear and everything you can think of.
Bye! Tanya

Maggie lowered the paper. "Looks like Tanya's dad's going to
keep her on a pretty short leash while they're here. I'll hardly
see her at all."

"Your friend has trouble with her father? He is extremely
strict?"

"Oh, well, not really. Well, yeah, but . . . he only tries to keep
an eye on her for her own good, I think. It's just that he overdoes
it, and she gets sneakier and sneakier the more he wants to know
where she is. It's kind of a hard thing for both of them." Maggie
could barely keep her mind on what she was saying, she felt so
let down. All Tanya really cared about was Paris glamour and
fashion. Even if she could have gotten permission to stay in
Paris longer, she would probably have had to be pulled bodily
from all the dumb clothing stores in order to do anything else.
Maggie lapsed into a moody silence, and when *Frère* Jacques
wandered over to her, she picked him up and hugged him close.

"Maggie?"

"What? Oh, sorry, Jean-Louis. It's just that . . ." She put *Frère*
Jacques down. "I guess I thought Tanya would come and help us
with our detective work, and the three of us would save Sr. Clare's

paintings from getting stolen and Tara from getting sold, and—it was just wishful thinking. A movie plot. A fantasy." She sighed heavily.

"Do not be sad, Maggie." Jean-Louis put his hand on her shoulder. "You and I are good detectives by ourselves. Someday they will write mystery books about our wonderful deeds!"

Maggie let the corners of her mouth turn upward into a smile. How could she stay down in the dumps with Jean-Louis around? "You're right. Neither an absentee sleuth nor a fake invalid can conquer us! What big celebration was Tanya talking about?"

"She is meaning Bastille Day. It is like your Fourth of July. We will have great fun that day!"

"Oh, good. I love Fourth of July at home, and this means I won't really miss it."

Her good humor restored, Maggie went to bed peacefully that night. But her subconscious must have still worried about Tara, because in her dreams an old lady without a face material-ized at the top of a hill, where she slowly opened a wet umbrella and held it over her head.

Straining to see, Maggie could not detect any signs of rain, but she could see Tara far behind the old lady. It lay beyond the hill in a low, mist-shrouded valley—elusive, beckoning.

Maggie tried to dodge around the bent figure and run toward her home, but the umbrella transformed into a shawl, and, hold-ing it with both hands, the old lady waved it in front of Maggie, blocking her way. Again and again, Maggie tried to get around the hunched figure to reach Tara. Yet again and again, the old lady and her shawl blocked the way.

11

La Boulangerie

IN THE MORNING, Maggie awoke exhausted—and late. Six-thirty. She should be downstairs at this very moment, meeting Jean-Louis and keeping an eye out for that scoundrel, Madame DuBois. She threw on a pair of shorts and a tee shirt and raced down the winding staircase and out into the courtyard sunshine. Good, she had beat Jean-Louis. She wandered around the courtyard trying to finish waking up and get the nightmare out of her head.

"*Frère* Jacques, where are you?"

The orange cat appeared at the top of the crypt steps. He took his time sauntering over to where Maggie waited for him in the middle of the courtyard, but snuggled right into her lap when she picked him up and went to sit on the presbytery steps. His steady purring helped settle Maggie's nerves.

Daylight and *Frère* Jacques eased the nightmare away, but the morning brought its own fear. Sr. Germaine had taught her how to ask for *baguettes* at the *boulangerie*, but Maggie still didn't want to go out into the city on her own. If only Jean-Louis would get here before Sr. Clare showed up. He could go with her.

The presbytery door opened behind Maggie, and she groaned into *Frère* Jacques's fur. Her aunt had beat Jean-Louis to the courtyard, and Maggie would have to go for bread alone.

"Good morning, Maggie." Sr. Clare sat down beside her and gave her a quick hug. "I'm glad for your sake that you're an early riser. It's the coolest part of the day. Are you ready for your first solo adventure?" She handed Maggie her cracked leather coin purse. "Maggie? Are you okay? You're looking a little pale." Her aunt put her paint-stained hand on Maggie's forehead. "No fever. Is something bothering you?"

At the concerned look on Sr. Clare's face, Maggie wanted more than anything to pour out all of her fears of the city and the terrible possibility of losing everything she loved, especially Tara. She longed to be comforted and reassured by this bulwark of a woman who looked as though she could handle anything. But the same thing that made Maggie want to confide in Sr. Clare held her tongue. How could she tell someone so confident and strong what a wimp she was?

"I'm okay," Maggie said lamely. "Just didn't sleep too great. I guess I'm not used to all the street noises yet."

Thankfully, Sr. Clare accepted that without question. "It is a big change from a small town, isn't it? The theaters and restaurants in this neighborhood do generate a lot of late-night noise. You'll probably get used to it and sleep fine in another couple days. Are you up for going to the *boulangerie* this morning?"

Maggie gulped. This was her chance to back out! But if she did, she'd probably stay a coward all her life, and her new father would wind up despising her, after all. Worse than that, she'd probably always hate herself. She forced the words from her lips.

"I'm fine," she said hoarsely, squeezing the coin purse so hard the clasp bit into her palm.

"*La Boulangerie,*" Sr. Clare reminded her. "It's written above the door, and it's exactly five blocks away. Don't get fooled and stop at *La Patisserie,* where you'll only find desserts. I don't want you spending our breakfast money on strawberry tarts!"

Maggie tried to smile. "I know. I made up a song about it last night when I was getting ready for bed. La Boo-lawn-jer-ee. I'll go to the right one." She put a protesting *Frère* Jacques down on the cobblestones and stood up. Pouch in hand, she marched toward the courtyard door.

"Ask St. Frances of Rome to accompany you," Sr. Clare called after her. "She's a patron Saint of traffic, and covers Paris as well as Rome!"

Maggie glanced over her shoulder as she opened the door. Another St. Francis? This time a woman? And a patron of traffic? Neat. "Okay. Bye."

To bolster her courage when she found herself alone on the sidewalk outside the courtyard, Maggie sang her way down the first block, devising tap steps as she went.

"*Patisserie—Boulangerie,*" she sang.

"They split 'em up, and woe is me!

One place for sweets and one for bread.

If I learn anymore, it'll break my head."

Sha-shuh, shuh, sha-shuh. Bop buh bop bop clackity clack, shuuuh-shah. Her feet slid along the sidewalk, rapped the pavement hard, and switched back to soft shoe.

"*Deux baguettes, s'il vous plaît*

Take my money; I'm on my way!"

It helped—for a while. The whole way to the bakery was on the quieter back streets, but by the third block, Maggie's shushing and clacking slowed to a snail-paced walk. When she spotted the sign that told her she had almost reached her goal, she heaved a great sigh of relief. *La Boulangerie.* In the middle of the next block, across the street. She had made it! The familiar tightness that squeezed the breath out of her in the city subsided. Air flowed into her lungs.

Maggie walked gratefully across the street to the little shop with the big window, nestled between a vegetable store and a fruit stand. She pushed the glass door of the *boulangerie* open and stepped into a room a third the size of Finch's Bakery. There were only two other customers in the shop, but when Maggie came in, she felt that she had entered a crowded room.

The other two customers, a couple of older girls, took their bags of rolls and went out the door, leaving Maggie alone to face the woman behind the counter.

"*Oui, Mademoiselle?*"

Maggie swallowed. She looked from the chunky clerk of some advanced age to the loaves of bread lining the shelves along the wall behind her. Back there, among brown and white round loaves, oblong short loaves, Kaisers, multi-grain buns and Russian black breads, the thin, two-foot loaves that Sr. Clare wanted leaned against the wall.

"Mademoiselle!" The clerk's sharp command pinned Maggie's feet to the floor.

"Deux baguettes, s'il vous plaît." In a hoarse whisper, Maggie managed the words Sr. Germaine had taught her.

The clerk's face puckered in her attempt to understand what Maggie knew must be an atrocious accent. "Ah," the woman proclaimed suddenly, and turned to pull down two of the long loaves. She wrapped each one around the middle with small squares of wax paper and handed them to Maggie. *"Deux francs, dix."*

Maggie gulped. Where had she heard those words before? What did they mean?

"Moh-nee." The clerk pointed at Maggie's clenched fist.

Maggie looked down at her hand. "Oh, yeah." She dumped all the change there was in the purse into the clerk's waiting palm.

The woman counted, nodded, and dismissed Maggie with a backhanded wave.

The walk home didn't seem so long, and Maggie only looked over her shoulder for wayward cars thirty or forty times.

Back in the courtyard, Jean-Louis sat waiting on the cement steps in front of the presbytery door. He stood when Maggie arrived.

"Soeur Clare told me where you had gone. How did you do with your errand?"

Maggie grinned triumphantly and held up the two long loaves the way Sr. Clare had the day before. "Piece of cake! Or, should I say, piece of *baguette?"*

Jean-Louis laughed and gave Maggie a quick hug that, for some reason, doubled her heart rate and sent her mind spinning.

"Here," she said to cover her confusion. "Hang onto this b*aguette* for us while I take the other one up to the Sisters, okay? Have you seen our suspect, Madame DuBois? Has grouchy old Gérard left from his night watchman work yet?"

"No, about our suspect. *Oui,* about Gérard.*"* Jean-Louis took the *baguette* and broke off an end piece. "He has gone, but you may not have escaped him all together. I think he will be back this morning to work with the crates for *Soeur* Clare."

"Rats, we'll have to dodge him all the time now." Maggie reached for the presbytery door, hesitated, and, holding the wrought iron handle, said, "Um, Jean-Louis, I've been thinking—about Gérard, I mean. Do you suppose it's possible that . . . oh, never mind; it's silly. I'll tell you later. Be right back."

— 12 —

Between the Walls

WHEN MAGGIE GOT downstairs from delivering the loaf of bread to Sr. Clare, she handed Jean-Louis a hunk of cheese and frowned down at him. "I knew it would happen," she said, sitting on the step beside him and accepting the half loaf of bread that he handed her. She took a bite and chewed as though it was the bread's fault that their plans were thwarted. "Sr. Clare said she needs our help upstairs this morning."

"Oh, that is too bad. Gérard has returned. He is down there." Jean-Louis pointed the remainder of his *baguette*-half toward the crypt stairs. "On his way to there, he looked at me as if to wish me dead. Perhaps he must clean away after the children again. Did they meet here last evening?"

"I don't know—maybe." Maggie fidgeted, feeling silly, but said what was on her mind anyway. "Jean-Louis, do you think that maybe—oh, man, this sounds dumb even to me—but, do you think Gérard might be up to something crooked?"

To Maggie's relief, Jean-Louis didn't laugh at her. "Hmm," he wiped breadcrumbs from the corner of his mouth, "it is possible, perhaps. But, Maggie," he raised his eyebrows, "I think Gérard is not smart enough for that."

"Well now . . ." That one took Maggie by surprise. "I hadn't thought of that, but I do have to admit you're probably right." She grinned. "Gérard's aunt must have him fooled as much as she does everybody else. Have you seen any sign of her?"

"Maggie! Jean-Louis!"

Maggie looked up. Nothing but blue sky and a couple of pigeons flying around. "I know I hear her. It's Sr. Clare, but where is she?"

"She is leaning from a window upstairs. We cannot see her, but she knows we are here." Jean-Louis stood up. "I may escort you up the stairs, *Mademoiselle?*" He ushered Maggie inside, and they headed up the stairs.

The next thing Maggie knew, she was standing in the kitchen holding one handle of a laundry basket full of wet sheets and towels. Jean-Louis had the other handle.

"Laundry day," Sr. Clare informed them needlessly. "You can be the hanger-uppers."

"She's worse than my mother for turning a vacation into forced labor," Maggie grumbled, only half meaning it, as she and Jean-Louis shuffled down the hall, the basket of clothes bobbing between them. They made a right turn at the pantry, and continued along the curving stone passageway that led past Sr. Clare's painting studio and office to a wooden door at the end of the passage. Maggie had been wondering what lay beyond that door. So there was at least one good thing about this job—she was about to find out.

"Be careful of your head and your feet," Jean-Louis warned. "The door is low, and there is a step down immediately. I have hit my head before, when carrying boxes here for the Sisters." He went first, and flicked the switch that turned on three low watt bulbs hanging from the rafters. The weak light illumined a bare room except for packing boxes stacked up along the sides and several clotheslines strung between the stone walls.

Maggie rubbed the toe of her sneaker over the sandy floor. "Did they always build basements in attics eight hundred years ago?"

"Perhaps, but this part of the presbytery is an addition. It is only three hundred years old. It is the church and the crypt under it that were built in the Middle Ages."

"Oh. Well, I'll tell you, this place is spooky. I bet there are spiders crawling all over the place—pre-historic ones—and bats." Maggie stuck clothespins on the sheets and towels almost faster than Jean-Louis could get them on the line, and ran for the door. "Come on, Jean-Louis!"

She slowed down once she got outside to the hallway, and Jean-Louis caught up with her.

"I will show you something very interesting, Maggie. Not even *Soeur* Clare knows I have discovered this." Carrying the empty laundry basket, he strode quickly past Sr. Clare's office-studio to the pantry.

Maggie watched, puzzled, as he put the basket down, picked up a flashlight from the little telephone table opposite the pantry, and continued straight to the hall wall in front of them. Maggie thought he would turn left, toward the kitchen, or right, toward the dining room, but, instead, he stopped, facing the blank wall.

"Do you see it, Maggie?" he said, turning to look at her.

Maggie came up beside him and squinted at the wall. See what? Some discolored paint? Oh, yeah, it's not discolored— it's a dent." She stooped to examine the spot in the wall more closely, running her hand over the concave surface. "A knob!" She straightened. "A hidden door?"

"*Oui.*" Jean-Louis's grin knew no bounds. "I have moved boxes to and from the storage room for the Sisters many times, and as a detective, I must keep aware of that which is around me. But, I have not yet been alone for enough time to explore what is behind the door. Do you wish to look now?" Without waiting for an answer, he opened the door and poked his head inside.

A musty, dead-mouse stench leaked out of the darkness.

"Yow!" Maggie held her nose, but peered beside Jean-Louis into the black hole. "Shoot, I can never see in the dark. Turn on the flashlight. Are there steps?"

"*Oui, escaliers!*" Jean-Louis said, shining his light upward, then downward, into the black hole. "The stairs are very . . ." he held his hands close together.

"Narrow," Maggie filled in for him.

"*Oui,* narrow. The steps make a circle in a very tight place— like an elevator shaft. They go uphill to the bell tower, I think, where only pigeons would go now. I do not know where the steps go at the bottom."

"Then we go down. Won't Tanya be sorry to miss this! It's like a corkscrew in here," Maggie said, gingerly testing the step just inside the doorway. "We'll have to go single file."

"I will go first, with the light. Stay close behind me, Maggie."
Jean-Louis didn't have to tell her twice. Shaking like Lou in *Abbott and Costello Meet Frankenstein,* Maggie entered the dark abyss as close behind Jean-Louis as bark to a tree. The flashlight threw fractured shadows onto the uneven stone walls. Her arm brushed against the wall's cold surface. "Yuk, slimy as worms in mud!"

"Be careful of slipping, Maggie. The steps are easy to slide on, because there have been many pigeons come into this place from the bell tower."

"How can you say that so calmly! Blaach!" Maggie had to force herself to keep her voice down to a whisper. She held onto the edges of the clammy stones in the wall in order to keep her feet from flying out from under her. "Ooh, hanging up the laundry at home was never like this."

After what seemed like years of slip-sliding down the goopy, pigeon-dung stairs, she and Jean-Louis reached the last step. Ahead of them stood a closed plank door.

"Now what? A dungeon? With dead people's bones in it?" Maggie shuddered.

"There is but one way to find out." Jean-Louis reached for the iron latch. "Ready?"

"Ready." Maggie didn't recognize the hoarse whisper that came from her throat.

Jean-Louis lifted the latch, and pushed hard. Maggie put her hand on his shoulder and leaned forward to see around him. The door swung open so easily, Jean-Louis fell headlong, and Maggie tumbled after him.

The flashlight flew out of Jean-Louis' hand and skidded several feet away along the cement floor. Maggie jumped up to retrieve it, but Jean-Louis scrambled to his feet quicker and beat her to it. She looked around.

"Bummers, it's only the church. There's the archway that leads into the presbytery and the courtyard—isn't it?" Maggie pointed directly to her left.

"*Oui.* The door has put us in the choir area, behind the altar. It is good they are not practicing at this moment! I am wondering . . ." Jean-Louis closed their door most of the way and stood back to examine it. "It is as I thought. Like the door upstairs, no person would notice this one, either. We have a wonderful secret, Maggie!"

"Fantastic!" Maggie gave Jean-Louis the thumbs up. "We'd better go back upstairs right away, so Sr. Clare doesn't start wondering where we are and find out."

"Yes, let us go quickly. No, wait!"

Maggie heard it as soon as Jean-Louis spoke. A man humming, and footsteps on the other side of the archway!

"My father—hide!" Jean-Louis pulled Maggie behind the wooden choir benches, the backs of which rose above them as they knelt in the cramped space between the back bench and the church wall.

Maggie winced when she looked to her left along the wall. They hadn't closed the secret door! Tense as a trapped fox, she stretched a little farther to watch a grownup likeness of Jean-Louis stride up to the choir director's podium, not ten feet in front of the choir benches. Only a little taller than Jean-Louis, he had the same curly black hair and lithe grace. His movements intense and purposeful, he was so focused on what he was doing, he didn't look anywhere except at the podium.

Good. Maggie quit worrying about the open door. She poked her head a few inches more around the end of the bench and watched *Monsieur* Gagnon snap up the papers that lay on the podium. Executing a crisp, military turn, he held up the paper in his hand and, staring at it as he left, broke into a new hum. The sound of it accompanied him through the archway and out the presbytery door.

Maggie turned to grin at Jean-Louis, but lost her balance in the tight space and fell against the wall. "Oops. Hey, this is nice—a wooden wall in our house of stone. But, it sure is flimsy." She ran her hand along the smooth, chipmunk-brown panel directly behind her and Jean-Louis. "See? It gave when I hit it, and now it jiggles when I push on it the least little bit. Pretty flimsy, all right."

"Flimsy? What is this word?" Jean-Louis slid the flashlight into his back pocket and ran his hand along the panel.

"Flimsy means wobbly, weak," Maggie said. "Give it a little push."

Jean-Louis did, and the panel wavered. "It is not like this church to have a wall so—flimsy," he said, frowning. "The choir place is new—maybe only two hundred years old. The early stone wall should be immediately behind the wood one. Perhaps . . ."

Still kneeling behind the choir bench, Jean-Louis scratched his head. He pushed on the wall again, this time in several places near him. The wood jiggled each time he put any pressure on it.

"Bartholomew wouldn't think too much of the workmanship on this wall," Maggie said, imitating Jean-Louis and pressing the wood here and there. "Flimsy everywhere."

"Hah!"

Jean-Louis's exclamation startled Maggie, but what happened next startled her even more.

"Yipes!" She grabbed Jean-Louis's arm. "Am I seeing what I think I'm seeing?"

"*Oui!*" Jean-Louis slid a narrow, three-foot high panel of the wall behind its adjacent panel. "A cupboard between two walls— as with the secret stairs. Except this space is very shallow."

"Probably chuck full of spiders and webs—eeeuw!" Maggie drew back as far as she could in the tight quarters between the wall and the choir bench.

"It does not look so," Jean-Louis said, reaching inside. "Ah!" He strained to pull something toward the opening.

"What is it? Let me see!"

"It is flat and stuck!" Jean-Louis's face reddened as he struggled to pull whatever he had hold of into the opening. He stopped, took a deep breath, and pulled again. "It is very difficult to move," he said, sweat breaking out on his forehead when he lugged the large object a few inches into the opening. "It is as high as my waist."

Maggie licked her dry lips. "It looks like a painter's canvas, Jean-Louis. Can you get it out any further?"

"I think you are right!" Jean-Louis exclaimed, edging the flat, square object a few more inches into the opening. "Perhaps it is one of Sr. Clare's! Perhaps someone is truly attempting to steal one of her paintings!"

"Galumpin galoobers, I can't stand the suspense! Look— brush marks!" Maggie stared at the series of red, yellow and orange brush strokes along the edge of the canvas Jean-Louis had managed to drag into the open.

"It is modern art!" Jean-Louis exclaimed, so excited he could hardly talk. "And I do not believe it is belonging to *Soeur* Clare. I believe it to be a Dumolin—the one I told you about—the last in the series of paintings stolen in Paris! Do you see the yellow of lightning and the red of fire? There is also the back of a head. It can be no other!" Jean-Louis grasped the edge of the canvas to pull it out farther. "Dumolin's modern figure compositions are the best in the world," he said, his back to Maggie.

Maggie shook her head, trying to rattle some sense into it. Until this second, she hadn't really thought of the whole thievery idea as real. But now . . . . "What should we do, Jean-Louis? If you're right, this is serious. What if . . . Oh, my gosh! Close the wall—quick!"

Jean-Louis obeyed instantly, and they both ducked low again.

More footsteps echoed faintly in the presbytery hall on the other side of the archway. The door to the courtyard creaked open, and Maggie could hear someone going outside, rather than coming into the church.

Not taking any chances, and connected by the same impulse, Maggie and Jean-Louis checked to make sure the wall panel was fully closed and ran for the secret stairs. They leaped into the murky darkness, pulling the door shut behind them. Squeezed together in the tight space, Maggie felt the cold, damp walls closing in on her.

"The flashlight, Jean-Louis! I can't see my own hand in front of my nose!"

"It is here, Maggie." Jean-Louis flipped on the light, and Maggie only realized she had been holding her breath when she gulped in a lungful of moist air.

"We've got to tell Sr. Clare, don't we?" she asked, when neither of them made a move to start up the narrow steps.

"*Oui,* it is important. But we will keep *les escaliers*—the stairs—a secret. Do you agree?"

"Definitely. We'd better get upstairs fast, though. Sr. Clare must think we've run away by now."

Maggie followed Jean-Louis up the mucky—those no-good pigeons—stone steps to the third floor, where they both scraped the bottoms of their shoes against the edge of a stone step. Jean-Louis leaned his ear against the door.

"I do not hear anyone," he whispered.

"Me neither. Let's go for it."

Jean-Louis pushed the door open, and they emerged into the apartment hallway.

Maggie felt as if she were stepping out of a time capsule. The empty laundry basket lay on its side by the pantry, exactly where Jean-Louis had left it. She picked it up, waited for him to return the flashlight to the telephone table, and walked with him to the kitchen.

"Just in time. Did you take a break?" Sr. Clare pulled a towel out of the littlest automatic washer Maggie had ever seen and dumped the towel on top of the pile in another basket. "It's all yours."

"Sr. Clare, wait! There's something important we have to tell you." Maggie stepped back from the full laundry basket.

"What is it, Maggie? You're tired of doing chores and want the afternoon off? Okay with me. You two are probably dying to do something besides hauling things and visiting the sick. Take the rest of the day off—*after* you've hung up this basket of laundry."

"Sr. Clare, this is serious!" With Jean-Louis's help, Maggie told Sr. Clare about the discovery of the hidden painting.

Sr. Clare eyed them both sternly. "If you two are playing some kind of joke . . . oh, what am I saying? That wouldn't be like either of you. I have to go see how Gérard is doing in getting started on the crates, anyway. We can take a look at your discovery at the same time."

On the way from the bottom of the main stairs to the archway that led into the church, Maggie, Jean-Louis and Sr. Clare passed the night watchman, who was coming in from the courtyard. He carried some large, flat boards under his arm.

"Ah, Gérard." Sr. Clare started talking with him in French, and, too impatient to hang around and listen to a lot of undecipherable chatter, Maggie motioned for Jean-Louis to come ahead.

"*Soeur* Clare has said that she will bring Gérard the measurements he needs in a few minutes." Jean-Louis explained as they

went through the archway into the church. Oh!" He grabbed
Maggie's arm. "The front door!"

Just before the door swung shut, Maggie caught sight of a
hunched brown-clad figure slipping away.

"Man-oh-man-oh-man." Maggie stumbled over her own
thoughts. "When did she . . . do you think she was here
when. . . ?"

"I do not think so, but . . ."

"Are you two going to stand there and mutter and stare at a
closed door all day, or show me your painting?"

Maggie jumped. She had been so intent on wondering what
Madame DuBois could have been up to that she hadn't heard Sr.
Clare coming.

Jean-Louis swung smoothly toward the choir area, bowing to
the altar as he passed it.

"*Mais, non, Soeur* Clare. We are ready. It is good that you
watch now. You will be happy to have come with us."

Maggie watched Sr. Clare watch Jean-Louis slide the wall
panel aside.

"Goodness!" Maggie's aunt exclaimed, "I had no idea about
that panel."

Maggie ran over to help Jean-Louis pull the painting out of
its hiding place, but stopped short when she saw the first few
inches of the canvas emerge from the cubbyhole.

Jean-Louis's mouth evolved in slow motion from an excited
grin to a shocked O as he gradually hauled the whole canvas
from the crevice and rested it against a solid part of the wall.

"My," Sr. Clare said, "it's a long way from a Dumolin, isn't it?
Hold it carefully, Jean-Louis, or the paint will crack."

"What happened?" Maggie couldn't move from where she
stood, halfway between her aunt and Jean-Louis. "It's impossible!"

13

Fake or Mistake?

THE CANVAS JEAN-LOUIS balanced on the floor in front of the sliding panel had reds and yellows and somebody's head in it, all right—but that's all the resemblance it bore to the one Maggie and Jean-Louis had seen earlier. The three kings following the star to Bethlehem. That's all this painting contained. There was the red of one of the king's robes. The back of his head. The gold of the star. And the painting was set in an ornate, old-fashioned frame.

"It's exactly the kind of old painting you'd expect to find in a cubbyhole like this," Sr. Clare said. "It looks familiar. I've seen it before. I wonder who painted it."

Maggie couldn't say a thing, and judging by Jean-Louis's shocked expression, neither could he.

"Well," Sr. Clare said after a long, awful silence, "it's an honest mistake, I'm sure. You did say you only saw a small part of the canvas, and in the dim light, and in your excitement, this could—I guess—look like a piece of modern artwork. Put it back so whomever it belongs to won't miss it, and let's go eat lunch."

"But, Sr. Clare!"

"Enough, Maggie. I have to give Gérard these measurements and talk to him about them, I'm hungry, and there's still a load of laundry to hang up before we eat." Sr. Clare started down the hall toward the unused office Gérard was using for his workroom.

"Oh, by the way," Sr. Clare called after Maggie, "you got an e-mail. I didn't have time to open or print it. You can check the "in-box" on your way back from hanging the laundry."

Deflated beyond speech, Maggie trudged up the stairs and into the kitchen apartment with Jean-Louis. Still unable to say anything, she took a handle of the full basket. Jean-Louis took the other one, and they started out of the kitchen.

Maggie's mind slowly moved from numb to functioning as she and Jean-Louis rounded the corner by the pantry.

"Oh, no!" She stopped in her tracks, almost dropping her end of the basket and causing Jean-Louis to jerk to a stop too.

"Maggie?"

"Don't you get it?" In her agitation, Maggie could hardly get the words out straight. "Sr. Clare went to her office, her studio—you know—when we were downstairs. That means she must have seen the laundry basket by the secret door. It's not a secret anymore, just when we really need it to help us find out what's going on here—without the help of any grownups! But now, Sr. Clare must know about the stairs. Oh, Rhett, all is lost!" Maggie laughed and groaned at the same time.

Jean-Louis ran a hand through his curly black hair. "Rhett?"

"He and Scarlett O'Hara are characters from a book called *Gone With the Wind.* It's one you probably haven't read yet. I'll explain it sometime. But right now, what are we going to do about Sr. Clare?"

"I do not think *Soeur* Clare is aware of the stairs, Maggie. She did not say anything about them to us. She did not even ask us what we were doing in the church to have discovered the hiding place. Perhaps she imagined I had to retrieve something there for my father. I do not know. But, she is very concentrated—like you saw with my father. I think that she would see only what she went to her office to see and not notice the laundry basket. She must have had a reason to use her e-mail. That is why she saw that you have a letter there. I believe we are safe."

"Oh, I hope you're right. Just the same, we'd better be lots more careful from now on!"

"With that, I agree with you, yes. Let us hang the towels very quickly, and see what it is that you have received."

"It's probably Tanya, raving about Paris fashions. Jean-Louis?" Maggie renewed her grip on the basket handle. "We did find a real painting, didn't we? We weren't excited and fooled by that thing we just saw?"

"No, Maggie. What we saw was a painting by Dumolin. This I know." Jean-Louis picked up his side of the basket again, and they walked with it toward the storage room. "Remember, Madame DuBois was leaving the church when we arrived there with *Soeur* Clare."

"Oh, yeah!" Maggie waited for Jean-Louis to open the storage room door. "I bet she made the switch and took the real painting in her shopping cart."

"*Oui*. It is too bad we did not see her cart. She would have had to balance the painting on top—and we would have known." Jean-Louis hung the towel Maggie handed him. "But even if we had seen a large object on her cart, there are more questions we cannot yet answer."

"Yeah, like, how did she come up with a substitute painting so fast? That's weird. Maybe it was farther back in the cubbyhole." Maggie lifted the now empty laundry basket. "Let's go look at the e-mail."

When they got into Sr. Clare's office-studio, Maggie opened the letter that awaited her on her aunt's computer. "Yep, it's from Tanya." She read the contents aloud.

> Dad's going to ask your aunt if you and she and the other two nuns you're staying with—and he said you could ask the boy you told me about too—could come for supper with us at a restaurant he knows in Paris.

"Oh, good, you're included too," Maggie interrupted herself, and then continued,

> That'll be on Sunday evening, July 15. Dad has to see your aunt while he's there, anyway, so he'll connect with her over supper. It'll be early and quick, though, because Dad said he'll be really tired after the trip and the big celebration on Saturday evening, so he wants to get to bed early on Sunday night. Our flight the next morning is at 6:30.

I say it's a good thing he wants to go to bed early!
That gives us a chance to have some fun and get more
time together in a way that really counts. Here's what
we'll do.

"Hoo, boy," Maggie interrupted herself again. "Tanya's up to her old tricks! What is it this time?" She read on:

Sunday after supper, we'll do as we're told. I'll go
back to the hotel with Dad, supposedly to go to bed.
You go back to the convent with your aunt. Your friend
can go back to his house, wherever that is. Then, you
two come to the hotel at midnight, and while Dad's
sawing logs in his room, you and your friend and I can
have a humdinger of a birthday party—on Dad's tab!

Maggie clapped her hand to her forehead. "Is she crazy? First of all, it's pure luck Sr. Clare didn't open this letter to print it for me. Even if she hadn't wanted to read it, she might have spotted this part. And there's no way she's going to let me out of here at midnight. What am I going to do?"

The answer hit them both at the same time. "The secret stairway!"

"But, Maggie, this is a joke, yes?" Jean-Louis's forehead creased into wrinkles. "She is not serious?"

"I wish she wasn't, but you don't know Tanya. She gets so many off-the-wall ideas." Maggie swung from alarm to guilty anticipation. If she had two cents worth of gumption to follow her own conscience, she'd write back this minute and tell Tanya to forget it, but . . . "Tanya will never forgive me, if I spoil Paris for her. Besides, it does sound pretty exciting. And," Maggie pulled out her best argument, "being out at midnight would give us a great chance to look for clues we might not find any other time."

Jean-Louis' solemn frown gave way to a grin. "You have won. I will do it! In my own city, I have never participated in a midnight party. It is time, no? But for now, we must go to eat lunch." He led the way out of Sr. Clare's office. "This afternoon we will return to Notre Dame Cathedral and the Left Bank, where we will look for Simon and ask if he has seen our main suspect—with a big parcel balanced on her cart!"

14

The Empty Room

TWO SECONDS AFTER finishing the lunch dishes, Maggie raced Jean-Louis down the staircase in the cavernous hallway, through the door at the bottom, and across the courtyard. One step ahead of him, she flung the wall door open and leaped onto the sidewalk.

"Freedom!" She broke into a rapid, heel-and-toe tap sequence, singing to her own rhythm. "Sr. Clare don't need us, don't want us, can't find us, won't see us. Get ready, Paris, here we come! Hey." Maggie stopped dancing and dropped her arms to her sides.

"What is it, Maggie? You look sick." Jean-Louis frowned.

"I just realized you'll be starting from your place, and I'll be starting from here when we sneak out to see Tanya that night." The thought of entering into the city alone after dark put a knot in Maggie's stomach that grew by the second. "Can you come and pick me up here?"

"But, Maggie," Jean-Louis said, looking puzzled, "that would be long for me. I will be coming from another direction. Ah . . . it will be very late in a strange city for you. We will work out a meeting place."

Maggie walked slowly across the street and down the block beside Jean-Louis. If only she weren't such a wimp, life would be lots easier.

"Can you come to the *boulangerie* alone?" Jean-Louis asked, three blocks later. He pointed to the little shop across the street.

Maggie nodded, relief flooding energy back into her body. She quickened her pace to keep up with Jean-Louis and, when they reached the teeming *Rue de Rivoli,* ran boldly across it with him.

They took the bridge to *Ile St. Louis* and approached the one that would lead them to *Ile de la Cité.*

"Great. Maybe I'll pick up a book to give Tanya."

"Your friend has mentioned in her letter a party," Jean-Louis said halfway across the second bridge. "This is her birthday?"

"Um, no, actually it's mine. I'll be fourteen the day we go to the hotel." Maggie didn't know why she blushed.

"Bon!" Jean-Louis put his arm around her shoulders. "That is a good reason for a party with your friend."

Flustered by Jean-Louis' enthusiasm, Maggie didn't know what else to say, but she decided that having her birthday so far away from home might not be so bad after all.

They arrived on *Ile de la Cité* and walked around to the front of Notre Dame Cathedral. Maggie gawked at the great structure like a regular star-struck tourist. She had gotten distracted from really seeing it the previous day, by spotting Simon, but now she gave the giant church her full attention.

"Wow," she breathed, "imagine building a place like this. Jean-Louis," she asked in a voice as hushed as she felt, "do you believe in God?"

"Oui, Maggie. When at first I began walking again, after the accident, I stopped inside this church often to rest and to talk to Him about what has happened." Jean-Louis absent-mindedly rubbed his thigh. "I have not come often now, though, because God has told me something that is very hard."

"Really? What?"

"He has asked me many times in my heart not to be angry with my father at his treatment of me. That is a very difficult request, and I am having much trouble with it. I *am* angry." The harshness that leaped into Jean-Louis' voice at his last sentence drifted into a sigh. "You see, Maggie, why I do not come here often now? I know that someday God will win our battle—He is much bigger and stronger than I am—but I am not ready for Him to win yet. Now, we will look for Simon, yes?"

"*Oui.* Let's go." Maggie wondered if Bartholomew was angry with Mr. Becker at how he was treating him, and if he argued with God about it. She stored Jean-Louis' words away where she could mull them over later, and brought her attention back to the task at hand. "Where do you think we'll find Simon?" She accompanied Jean-Louis across the street to the stretch of grass heavily populated by artists and onlookers.

"He is not here," Jean-Louis said ten minutes later. "We can continue to the Left Bank. Later we will try here again."

"Okay." She went with Jean-Louis across the first bridge past Notre Dame Cathedral that would take them from the island to the Left Bank. "There it is," she said a couple blocks and around a corner later. "Shakespeare and Company. I feel at home there already—and I've only been in it once. And that time," she said, panting in the heat, "they didn't have Rip Van Winkle as an outside decoration. Look who's lazing on a bench over by the door. Hey, Simon!"

Starting at the sound of his name, Simon unfolded his long, crossed legs and stood. He looked around, and, blinking sleepily, finally saw them. "Oh, hi there. I was hoping to run into you two soon." The tall, loose-jointed artist strolled over to Maggie and Jean-Louis, a sketchpad tucked under one arm. "How you doing?"

"Fine and dandy," Jean-Louis said in his expanding English. "Why are you here, not at Notre Dame?"

"Check this out." Simon drew them back over to his bench. When Maggie and Jean-Louis were seated on either side of him, he opened his sketchbook.

"You're kidding—this is inside the bookshop?" Maggie couldn't believe her eyes. "Not only can she walk, she must be able to read English, too. She's a double phony! What's that painting in the book she's looking at?" Maggie bent more closely over Simon's detailed drawing. "Jumpin' catfish!" She clapped her hands together. "It's the painting that's hanging in the Becker's living room! Sr. Clare's painting! What's it doing in that book?"

"It's an anthology of modern art," Simon said. "Here's the name of it. He handed her a slip of notepaper. "I copied the title down when the lady left, and stuck the book on the bottom shelf of the first row of fine art books."

"That's great, Simon—you're the best!" Maggie looked at the title. *"Art and Artists in the Last Quarter of the Twentieth Century,"* she read, "by a fellow whose name I can't pronounce."

"You have done well," Jean-Louis said, looking up from the sketch for the first time.

"Well, hey," Simon said, shrugging, "I enjoyed the drawing practice. Besides, it was a good challenge—balancing on one of those rolling ladders that allow you to reach books on the top shelf. That way, I could see the lady and her book, but she didn't notice me behind her. 'Course, I don't think she would have noticed it if I had fallen off the thing and into her lap, she was so concentrated on her reading. Lucky for me, she kept on the same page for a while."

Maggie laughed, but her mind was on what Madame DuBois could possibly be up to, and not on how she had kept Simon entertained.

"We know that painting of Sr. Clare's isn't in jeopardy," she said, "because it's hanging safely on the Becker's wall. And you said the stolen paintings have always disappeared on their way to the gallery where they're supposed to end up, Jean-Louis."

"That is true," Jean-Louis nodded. "But there may be other patterns in the thefts that we do not yet know about. We must do research. For this, I need French. Tomorrow is Sunday, but on Monday we must go to the Beaubourg—the Pompidou Center."

"Well, this has all been fun, guys," Simon said, yawning widely, "but I have to get back to my real money-making sketching. See you around." Simon tore the page with his latest drawing of Madame DuBois from his book. "You can have this as another souvenir. Bye."

"Thanks!" Maggie accepted the paper gingerly. "I'll put it up beside your other one in my room."

"Wait, Simon!" Jean-Louis swung in front of Simon to stop him. "We still need you to help us." He rapidly told Simon everything, from the midnight meeting with Tanya to the painting that had disappeared from its hiding place.

"That's interesting, all right," Simon said. "There's probably some logical explanation for whatever happened, but okay—I'll hang in there with you for a while. What is it you want me to do?"

"Can you perform a drawing of anyone else you see with Madame DuBois?" Jean-Louis asked.

"Especially," Maggie said, rolling up her sketch and glancing defensively at Jean-Louis, "of Madame DuBois's nephew, Gérard. He's the night watchman at the church and convent."

"That is good, Maggie." Jean-Louis smiled enthusiastically. "You are right that we must not dismiss anyone too quickly. Simon?"

Simon shook his head, but relented. "You two are something else, but, sure, why not? Come back around here or around Notre Dame in a few days, and we'll reconnoiter."

"Thanks, Simon. You're terrific." Maggie restrained herself from throwing her arms around the lanky artist.

"*Oui,* you are a valuable helper." Jean-Louis shook Simon's hand, and stood up.

Maggie shook the artist's hand and got up, too. "Bye," she said and went inside the shop with Jean-Louis. She handed him the paper with the book title on it and went to look for a book for Tanya. Half an hour later, when she had decided that Tanya was bound to like the written version of *Pride and Prejudice,* since she had loved the video, Jean-Louis came and pulled her away from the Victorian novel section.

"Come. You will be interested to see." He led her to a table where a large book lay open. "This is the picture by *Soeur* Clare. And look at this one." Jean-Louis flipped back several pages to another print.

Seeing the print he had turned to, Maggie couldn't even come up with an appropriate exclamation. "I'm struck speechless," she said. Look, it's all there. The reds, the gold, the browns. The back of that man's head. It has to be the one. It's the Dumolin, isn't it?" Maggie looked from the print to Jean-Louis. "Do you think she might have really stolen that one, and now she's after one of Sr. Clare's? Should we call the police?"

"I do not know." Jean-Louis flipped back and forth between the Dumolin print and the one of Sr. Clare's painting. "What would help them to believe us? We have told Simon everything we know, and he still does not believe us. I can tell. Sr. Clare thinks we were excited children who made a mistake in what they saw. No, we have no evidence to show the police yet, but I think we are adding up more pieces of what you have said is a very large puzzle." Jean-Louis put the bound volume on a shelf that held lots of similar art books. "It is getting late. We must go to the hotel now. From there, we will walk back to the *boulangerie,* and I will leave you to go to my home. This is all right for you?"

"Sure, no sweat, there'll still be lots of daylight. Good practice."

Maggie felt brave at the moment, but by the time she actually got back to the bakery, and Jean-Louis waved goodbye, she gulped—and ran the whole way back to the convent. Safely inside the courtyard, she knew it was almost suppertime, and she should keep moving, but she took a couple minutes to sit on the presbytery steps and catch her breath before going on upstairs.

When she did get upstairs, she found Sr. Clare in the kitchen. "Did you know Richard Becker is coming in a couple weeks?" her aunt asked after first inquiring how her afternoon had been.

Maggie nodded. "Tanya wrote to tell me."

"Thought she might have. Richard wrote me that he's bringing his daughter. He wants to give her a chance to see Paris, but this trip is a real blitz—forty-eight packed hours, including the time they'll need for recovering from jet lag. Richard is inviting us to have supper with them on their second evening here. Jean-Louis is invited as well. It will be exciting for you to see someone from home, I expect, even though for so short a visit."

Maggie did her best to act casual. "Yep, it will. I'm really looking forward to seeing Tanya."

"Good." Sr. Clare pulled a square baking dish out of the oven and put it on top of the stove. "I told Germaine I'd give her a break and make supper today, but relax, I'm not making toast!

"I'm not looking forward to meeting with Richard when he comes," Sr. Clare continued as though speaking to an adult equal and jabbing a fork into a piece of chicken in the dish. "He'll probably have plenty to say—not good, of course—about the slides I sent him of the paintings that will be in the exhibit."

Maggie tried to think of something mature and wise to say about her aunt's predicament, but she couldn't come up with anything, and it didn't seem to matter, anyway. Sr. Clare didn't pause long enough for a response.

"There's no way getting out of seeing him," she said, putting a lid on the chicken dish and sliding it back into the oven. "Richard will be accompanying the paintings back to Ft. Wayne, and I want to personally hand him the forms Sr. Thérèse has helped me fill out for him." She pulled the breadbasket down from the top of the cupboard. "Here, could you help me with this?"

Maggie took the basket and wrapped some slices of Italian bread in the red-and-white checkered towel.

"Here's the salad, too. Can you handle both? Good. Let's get this food into the dining room before the others think we've taken off to the Yukon with it." Sr. Clare led the way to the dining room.

"How's Gérard coming along with the crates?" Sr. Thérèse asked, reaching for a slice of bread after grace.

"He'll have to work hard for the next ten days, in order to finish on time," Sr. Clare said, "but he doesn't want any help. Claims help would take him longer!"

"He works hard, more hard for him."

Maggie smiled at Sr. Germaine's hint that sustained physical labor was a major change for Gérard.

"He is happy that your show will be in the United States?"

Sr. Clare shrugged. "He does seem to be, Germaine."

Maggie ate her chicken in silence, wondering if she should slip downstairs after dishes to see if Madame DuBois was around.

"How about teaching us that card game you told us about, Maggie?" Sr. Clare said, breaking into, and seeming to respond to, Maggie's thoughts. "You know, 'Hand and Foot'? The dishes can wait for a change."

Maggie blinked at her aunt. Oh no, not now! "Uh, sure. Okay. Do you have enough decks of cards?"

"Of course. I borrowed some from Fr. Francois this afternoon. I'm long overdue for a relaxed evening. How about you, Germaine? Thérèse?"

"I'll do my best, for the sake of community." Sr. Thérèse kept a polite, straight face, but Maggie grimaced on her behalf. Poor Sr. Thérèse. She hadn't looked like the card-playing type.

"Good for you, Thérèse—I knew you had it in you to learn how to relax." Sr. Clare turned to the golden nun. "Germaine?" *"Mais, oui.* I will do battle." Sr. Germaine cleared the dishes from the table and stacked them on the side cupboard.

Trapped by her own earlier suggestion, Maggie accepted the five decks of cards Sr. Clare held out to her.

By the time the game ended and they did dishes and left the kitchen apartment, it was late, dark and overwhelmingly quiet in the big hall.

"Gérard must be on his rounds," Sr. Clare said, leaning way out over the stairway banister. "No light down there. I'll wait until tomorrow to see how he's doing on the crates." She unlocked the door to the chapel apartment. "Bedtime, Maggie. Thanks for the lesson. We'll play again soon so we don't forget all we learned."

"Great." Maggie pulled her attention away from the shadowed depths of the presbytery stairwell and followed the Sisters into the apartment.

"Goodnight, Maggie. Goodnight, everybody." Sr. Thérèse turned into her room.

"Bonne nuit. Merci, Maggie." Sr. Germaine hugged Maggie and turned into her room, across from Sr. Thérèse.

"'Night, Maggie. Sleep well." Sr. Clare hugged Maggie too and waited until Maggie had gone the rest of the way down the hall to her own room, opened her door and flipped on the light. Then she waved and disappeared into her own room.

Maggie sat on the edge of her bed, letting random thoughts run through her head. What *had* happened to the Dumolin painting? Tomorrow was soon enough to start tailing Madame DuBois again. Sr. Thérèse was one funny card player. For somebody who spoke umpteen languages and probably knew enough to write her own encyclopedia, she couldn't remember how many points a king or an ace was worth. Maybe Sr. Clare was right. Maybe Sr. Thérèse had been so busy learning other things she had never had time to learn how to play. Poor Sr. Thérèse.

Maggie sighed, and realized how tired she was. She stumbled into pajamas, brushed her teeth, and fell into bed.

She awoke at six on the nose, sunlight filling her room. Perfect. Dressing quickly, she started running down the ninety-nine steps in the dim hall, ready to meet Jean-Louis and work out their next plan of action in solving "The Mystery of the Missing Dumolin," she said aloud halfway down the stairs. "Yeah, good title for a new movie. I'll have to see if Jean-Louis likes it."

At the ground floor level, the hallway didn't feel as though it had awakened yet. It lay dark and quiet—except for a single beam of light that streamed into the corridor from the narrowly opened door of the room Gérard was using to make the shipping crates.

Bingo! Maggie tiptoed down the hall and peeked inside the room.

Two sawhorses. Scattered piles of sawdust. A makeshift wooden counter. Some single pieces of board leaning against the right-hand wall. A power saw on the counter. A few huge wooden boxes shaped like overgrown sandwiches leaning against the far wall. Nothing more. Rats, the place looked like any basement carpentry shop. Nothing weird or suspicious about it. Maggie took a step inside. Another. She moved toward the nearest crate, and reached out to touch it.

"Ne touchez pas!"

Maggie leaped back.

Gérard barreled down on her like a miniature tornado, coffee splashing out of a steaming mug in his hand. Maggie ducked away from him and ran for the door, a volley of fast-flung French pushing her. The door slammed shut at her heels.

⟶⟍⟍ 15 ⟋⟍⟶

Tap Dance into Trouble

MAGGIE WASN'T SURE her feet even touched the floor as she took off down the hall and jerked the door open at the end. She flew down the cement steps and into the courtyard.

"Maggie! What is it?" Jean-Louis ran toward her from the outer wall door.

"I . . . he . . ." Maggie tried to catch her breath and her wits. "That Gérard is mean enough for a person ten times his size!" She told Jean-Louis what had happened.

"That is most interesting!" Jean-Louis said, shifting his weight to his strong side. "Do you know who now sits in the church? I walked around the complete park this morning, to look at what I could find, and I saw her cross the street and enter by the main door."

"Madame DuBois—and she might have heard Gérard chase me out of his workroom! Do you think she came here to meet him?"

"I do not know. But we must part. If you hide in the parish kitchen, you will be able to know if Madame DuBois and Gérard meet inside. I will return to near the front door of the church to see if she comes out again at that spot."

Before Maggie could protest, Jean-Louis ran across the courtyard and out the door. There was nothing left to do but slip back inside the presbytery and into the empty kitchen. "If Gérard catches me here, I'm dead meat," she groaned, peeking around the doorway barely enough to see the hall and the archway to the church.

The presbytery door banged open, sending Maggie a mile into the air, and Jean-Louis ran into the kitchen.

"Come quickly!"

Her heart in her throat, Maggie ran after him to the court-yard. "What is it?"

"I must go," Jean-Louis said breathlessly. "Madame DuBois is walking away. You stay to watch Gérard."

"No, not fair! What if he comes out here?" Maggie didn't want to be alone in the same country with the night watchman, never mind in the same courtyard. But she knew Jean-Louis was right. It couldn't be the other way around. For her to go out into the city, not knowing where she would end up, would be crazy. "Okay, go," she said, "but get back here as soon as you can!"

Maggie spent the next half hour pacing the courtyard and chewing her fingernails. If Gérard came out and saw her, he would blast her from here to Indiana. But, in time to spare her and save her last four fingernails from annihilation, Jean-Louis finally returned. He swung over to where she had stopped pacing, in the middle of the courtyard, and talked fast.

"Madame walked with her cart to the Seine," he said, brushing beads of sweat from his forehead. "There she fed the pigeons crumbs. After this, she went home." Jean-Louis lifted his shoulders and dropped them again. "A dead end, as you would say."

"Bummers. Where is all this leading us? I'm more and more sure she and Gérard are in cahoots. They're so cagey. Gérard hasn't shown his face in the courtyard once since you left. What can we do that will *get* us somewhere?"

"We are one step more than before," Jean-Louis said. "I have seen Simon—on the bridge that leads to *Ile St. Louis*. Madame DuBois had turned to walk away from the river, and before I continued to follow her, I talked one moment with Simon. He did not seem very awake, but he has been near the courtyard last night, and he is knowing what Gérard looks . . ."

Listening intently to Jean-Louis, Maggie jumped at the creaking of the presbytery door behind her. It swung open, and Gérard stepped outside. Maggie held her breath.

From the top of the low set of steps, the little night watchman scowled out at Maggie and Jean-Louis. "Shah!" He marched down the steps and headed toward them, his short legs churning. Two inches in front of them, he stopped long enough to spit a barrage of French at Jean-Louis, and then stormed past them.

"What'd he say?" Maggie asked as soon as the courtyard door swung closed behind the bad-tempered little man.

"He said that he is warning us not to go near the room where he is making the . . ."

A car door slammed and a motor revved up. Jean-Louis grinned. "You stay here in the case that he returns. I will go inside." Jean-Louis went into the presbytery, but arrived back in two seconds. "It is locked."

"Rats. Now what?"

"Now I must go home to change my clothes and prepare for Mass at St. Gervais. My father has accepted to be the choir director there today, because their usual director is sick. It works well, because the children's choir is singing here, and someone else directs them."

"Too bad. That means I won't get to meet your parents yet. Oh, well, later. I'm going to the early Mass here with the Sisters, then Sr. Clare is going to teach me to paint with acrylics, and they're all taking me for a picnic near a place they called Montmartre, that overlooks the city. The rest of this day is shot, as far as sleuthing goes."

"*Oui,* but you will like Montmartre. It has many more sidewalk artists and a beautiful church at the top of the mountain. Tomorrow I will meet you here, and we will go to the Beaubourg, where you will see the gallery of art, and I will study the French library to see if I can locate translations of the newspaper articles you mentioned to me, and to see what more is to be found out about the stolen paintings."

—◦◦◦—

"I was correct!" Jean-Louis exclaimed the next morning as soon as he opened the door to let Maggie out of the Beaubourg—

the Pompidou Center. "There *are* other patterns concerning how the paintings have been stolen! For example, each painting was a new one—on its way to a gallery for the first time." Hardly looking where he was going, he talked excitedly about the five known thefts all the way back to the church.

"So you see," he said, leading the way through the wall door of the courtyard, "according to his articles, Art Brandenshaw—your Bartholomew—suspects that the stolen paintings are all connected to each other—possibly the work of one smuggling ring. And *I* suspect that this group of criminals may attempt to steal one of *Soeur* Clare's paintings. We must find out what Madame DuBois has done with the Dumolin painting!"

"Good work, Jean-Louis—we're on a roll! Bartholomew can't possibly be one of the thieves, writing those kinds of things about them. The more solid information we dig up, the quicker Mr. Becker will have to let up on him, and Tara will be safe! I'll go tell Sr. Clare we're home, then we can plan what to do about Madame DuBois."

On her way back from reporting in to her aunt, Maggie felt so good about how things were going, she tap- danced the whole second half of the way down the long, winding staircase.

"Crack this case and land those crooks," she chanted. "Bap, rap, tickety-slap!" Her feet hit the stairs—down one, up two, back down three. Maggie leaped the last three steps and landed in the hall. Out of breath, but not willing to quit dancing, she tapped in the opposite direction down the hall from the presbytery door, meaning to reach that end, then propel herself the whole length of the hall to a grand finale at the door, where she would jump out to meet Jean-Louis.

In great form, she danced down the back end of the hall. Just before she reached the end, she heard the presbytery door open behind her.

"What are you doing, Maggie? Oh, that looks fun!"

Maggie twirled around to see Jean-Louis dancing, sliding, swinging toward her. His natural grace compensated for his injured leg and made for some never-seen-before innovative steps.

Maggie laughed and tapped to meet him. They met in the middle, at the bottom of the stairs, and grasped hands, swinging around in a square-dance finish.

"Good going, Jean-Louis!"

"And you, Maggie. Someday we must both take lessons! Look, they dance too." He pointed at an old painting on the wall between Gérard's workroom and another office.

Maggie looked at the dancing couple in the painting. The woman had on a long, flowing gown, and the man wore some sort of Victorian finery. The picture reminded her of something else she had seen recently. In an instant, she knew what it was.

"Jean-Louis, do you think . . ."

"*Oui,* let us search!" No longer dancing, Jean-Louis started down one side of the back part of the hall, and Maggie took the other side.

"*Ici,* Maggie! Come!"

She ran over to him, and sure enough, where a picture should be hanging near the very back of the hall, there was only an empty space, much cleaner than the rest of the wall around it.

"Let's see if it's the right size!" Maggie danced on tiptoe outside the first floor parish kitchen while Jean-Louis ran in to get a piece of string out of the utility drawer, and then both of them ran through the archway into the church. Empty, thank heavens. Inch by inch, they tugged the medieval painting from the cubbyhole. Halfway into the open, the canvas broke free of what turned out to be a broken piece of wood wedged between the picture frame and the inner wall. Once it broke free, the painting slid out easily.

Jean-Louis snatched up the wood and examined it. "This has been broken recently," he said, holding it up for Maggie to see and looking carefully over the old frame they had just pulled into the open. "It is not part of this painting."

"Evidence!" Maggie whispered. "At least, maybe. Hang onto it, Sherlock!"

Jean-Louis pocketed the piece of wood.

"Good! Now, let's get this thing measured and back into hiding before anyone comes." Maggie held the canvas while Jean-Louis quickly measured the length and width of it. As soon as he was finished, the two of them shoved the old picture back into its cubbyhole. Halfway in, it resisted, but a little jiggling and lifting got it all the way back into place.

Moving as one, Maggie and Jean-Louis ran back into the hallway and measured the empty space on the wall. The two dimensions matched exactly.

"'The Wise Men' goes here, all right," Maggie said. "The only question now is," she searched the wall in front of them, "where is the Dumolin paint . . ."

"Dance, Maggie!" Still holding the piece of string, Jean-Louis grabbed her hands and started dancing toward the presbytery door.

Maggie guessed what had happened at the same time that she heard Gérard's angry shouts.

"Do not stop, Maggie!" Jean-Louis danced her toward the door through which Gérard had just entered the presbytery, and they whirled past the red-faced night watchman, almost tripping him and themselves on their way out the door.

"What was he yelling at us?" Maggie asked, collapsing at last onto a bench in the park.

"He was saying many things about children and what demons they are in words I will not translate to a girl." Jean-Louis wove the string around his fingers with a flourish. "The empty wall space and the piece of wood—these are wonderful clues. Do you have a camera, Maggie?"

"Yeah, sure, my mom made me bring her old instamatic. It's still in my suitcase. Why do you . . . oh, I see—document the evidence! Be right back." She ran upstairs for the camera, and they took pictures of their two pieces of evidence.

"This is superior, Maggie," Jean-Louis said, putting the broken piece of wood back into his pocket. "Two clues in one morning. Others will come quickly now!"

That night, behind her closed bedroom door, when Maggie photographed Simon's two sketches of Madame DuBois, she felt confident, too, that they were on a clue-gathering roll.

Unfortunately, they were both wrong. The next ten days held a whirlwind of activities for Maggie:

A train trip with Jean-Louis and the Sisters to Giverny, where the Impressionist painter, Claude Monet, had lived and painted his famous pictures of water lilies.

An exploration of the tree-lined, café-lined *Avenue Des Champs Elysées* that began at one end with Napoleon's monumental *Arc de Triomphe.*

An English movie—*The Hound of the Baskervilles*—at a small neighborhood theater older than the Roxy.

Painting lessons in the park with Sr. Clare.

Gathering postcards for her mom and Bartholomew to show them all the places she was discovering.

Sending and receiving e-mails from them and Tanya.

Touring more of downtown Paris and learning about the upcoming Bastille Day—an equivalent of America's Fourth of July.

But no more clues.

"Let's go see if we can find something good to read at Shakespeare and Company," Maggie said two days before Bastille Day and Tanya's arrival in Paris. "It's so hot and sticky, I don't feel like doing anything else, and no crook in his right mind would be planning any big jobs today."

"*D'accord.* I agree. And after the English bookstore, I will treat you to an Italian *gelato.*"

Maggie packed up her paints, and Jean-Louis rose lazily from the park bench.

"After Bastille Day," he said, "when it becomes even hotter, and especially in August, there will be no one left in Paris except tourists and those who must stay to take care of them. Everyone else will escape to the beach."

"Smart move, I'd say." Maggie wiped fruitlessly at her dripping forehead.

At the bookshop on the Left Bank, she ignored the sticky heat and scrounged through the bulging shelves and found an old, much-handled copy of *Wuthering Heights.* "Perfect for a long, hot day in which we still haven't turned up one measly clue about our missing painting," she told Jean-Louis, who ambled over to her aisle. "It's a Victorian tragedy. What did you find?"

"A volume of three mysteries by a person called G. K. Chesterton," he said. "Father Brown is the same detective in all three."

"You have a one-track mind," Maggie said, laughing. "Where do we go for ice cream?"

"Very near to here—maybe three or four blocks. Let us go to pay for our books, and I will take you there."

Maggie started down the aisle toward the cashier's desk just as Simon burst into the shop through the front door. Startled, the two suited, elderly gentlemen, lined up to pay for their purchases, stepped backward in unison.

Simon didn't seem to notice. He poised suspended, his tall, lanky form bent forward, searching. He caught Maggie's eye, and his face lit up. "Ah!" The pages of his sketchpad flapping under his arm, he ran over to where she and Jean-Louis stood as transfixed as the cashier and the two customers at the front desk.

"Wait 'til you guys see this!" Simon's excited stage whisper turned more heads in their direction. "Sorry," he whispered loudly to the room at large. He took Maggie's arm and nudged Jean-Louis toward the door.

"We have to pay for our books," Maggie said frantically, "or the cashier will be coming outside with us!"

"Oh, okay, I'll wait for you." Once he seemed to realize Maggie and Jean-Louis weren't going to disappear on him, Simon left as casually as if he had simply wandered into the shop to browse.

Maggie blinked. "Was he really here?"

"*Oui*, and he must have a very good clue for us. Hurry!"

Maggie wiped her sweating face, wondering how she could be so hot yet have a cold shiver of excitement run through her at the same time.

Outside the bookshop, Simon pulled her and Jean-Louis over to an empty bench. "You won't believe what happened! There I was, hanging around Notre Dame and here all week, making some pretty good money doing street sketches and keeping an eye out for your friend. She never showed up, of course, and I almost forgot about her, so, I thought I'd take a break today and wander around—you know, check out a few galleries to see what's new—that sort of thing?"

Simon snatched a quick breath and went on. "So, there I was, my mind on art and a good cup of coffee. I sniffed the air and found a great new sidewalk café right across the street from *Musée Millénaire Nouveau* that serves superb coffee, so I hung out there for a while. I thought maybe I'd sketch the place and then. . ."

"Simon!" Maggie shook his arm, and Jean-Louis clapped his hand over Simon's mouth.

"I will let go only if you will inform us about what you have discovered in fewer than one thousand words!"

"Mmphglph!" Simon shook free and opened the sketchpad on his lap.

"Check this out." He held the open pad at an angle so that Maggie, on his left, could see it.

"It's Gérard!" Maggie exclaimed. "But who's the brute with him? What a face—I wouldn't want to run into him in a dark alley!"

Jean-Louis leaned over Simon's other shoulder to get a look at the sketch too.

"*Mais,* Simon!" he gasped, and babbled animatedly in French, pointing first at the building behind Gérard in the sketch, then at the other figure.

"You got it!" Simon broke into French too, talking as wildly with his hands as he did with his words. Maggie got dizzier and dizzier.

"Stop it!" She glared at them. "I want to know what's going on!"

Jean-Louis looked blankly at Maggie. "Mais . . . but . . . ah! I am sorry, Maggie," he said, switching to English. "Do you see? Gérard and this man—he is in the uniform of a museum guard—are standing in front of . . ."

"*Musée Millénaire Nouveau!*" Maggie finished for him. "I get it!" Her feet tapped an excited rhythm against a leg of the bench. "Your research at the Beaubourg is paying off. You said the Dumolin wasn't the only painting that disappeared on its way to the *Musée.* So did one by some fellow named Rico—three years ago. Right? Yo, doggies!" Maggie's mind shot to the next conclusion, but Jean-Louis beat her to saying it.

"Art Brandenshaw—Bartholomew—*must* be correct to guess that one smuggling ring is perhaps involved in all the thefts, and Gérard and Madame DuBois must be part of the ring!" Jean-Louis smiled broadly.

"Yes!" Maggie jumped in again. "Simon, you've got to keep tailing Gérard as well as Madame DuBois now. This is fantastic, what you've got here. Three suspects, and counting!"

"Maybe." Simon leaned nonchalantly against the backrest of the bench and flipped to the next page in his sketchbook. "Take a gander at this before you draw too many conclusions."

Maggie and Jean-Louis looked over Simon's shoulders at the new sketch, or, actually, two sketches on the page he showed them.

"I don't get it," Maggie said, after a long silence. "It's obvious in the top drawing that the old lady wrapped up in her shawl at the café table is Madame DuBois trying not to be recognized, but . . ."

Jean-Louis pointed at the lower sketch. "In this drawing, she is sneaking away in one direction, Gérard is going away in the opposite direction, and the guard is going back into the museum." Jean-Louis scratched his head. "Perhaps Madame DuBois and Gérard meet together later?"

"Nope." Simon flipped the sketchbook closed. "Just for the heck of it, I tailed Madame DuBois for the next forty-five minutes. All she did was wander over to Notre Dame Cathedral, then across the river to an apartment building in the Sisters' neighborhood that must be where she lives. When she went inside, I left and came back over this way. That was yesterday."

"Maybe Gérard was doing some kind of legitimate business for Sr. Clare, and Madame DuBois was spying on him." Maggie slowly tapped one foot against the bench leg, and remembered the camera hanging around her neck by its strap. "Could we get a couple shots of your sketches, Simon?"

"You getting lessons from Scotland Yard now?" Simon dutifully turned back a page and held the sketchbook up so Maggie could get a good angle. "Lucky for you guys, I'm the agreeable type." He turned back to the two sketches of Madame DuBois, and Maggie got a shot of that page too.

"We are at least aware that another person might be involved in this case," Jean-Louis said, when Maggie finished and down again. "Is it possible that you can watch for him, too, Simon?

"Sure, no sweat." Simon tucked his sketchpad under his arm and stood. "It's an interesting diversion. Why don't we rendezvous here at Shakespeare and Company Saturday afternoon at two o'clock. That's the day before your big midnight party, isn't it? Hey, do you realize that'll be Bastille Day? I'll have sketching to do—money to make—that day! Oh, well, I can free up some time to meet you. Two o'clock, then. We'll see what we see by then."

———⌘———

The first thing Maggie saw when Bastille Day came around was that between the excitement of the national holiday and the hope of getting more news from Simon, she was wound up tighter than a top ready to spin.

It seemed that the whole city of Paris rang with the sounds of celebrating—music playing everywhere, people talking excitedly in groups that bumped into each other as they moved in and out of buildings and along the sidewalks, little kids laughing, licking ice cream cones, and chasing each other around in circles.

At ten-thirty in the morning, Jean-Louis rushed Maggie to *Rue de Rivoli,* where military planes of every shape and size roared close overhead along the path of the street, trailing plumes of red, blue and white smoke.

In the Latin Quarter, on the Left Bank, Maggie ate her first meal—a gelled salad with a boiled egg in the middle—outdoors at a sidewalk café.

"That was great," she said, washing it down with a good old American coke. "We're going to have to hurry to get to Shakespeare and Company in time to meet Simon at two."

"It is not far from here," Jean-Louis said, pushing his chair back. "I will pay—and we will run!"

They got there at two sharp.

"I can hardly believe Tanya's in Paris now," Maggie said, watching a group of three people get up from the bench where she and Jean-Louis had met with Simon two days earlier. She ran over to the vacated bench. "Poor girl, wasting all this time sleeping off jet lag." Maggie fidgeted on the bench. "Where's Simon?"

"There's something fishy about Gérard and that guard, for sure," Simon said, appearing on cue from behind a collection of customers looking at the books in the shop's outdoor stalls. He landed on the bench between Maggie and Jean-Louis. "They were hanging around outside the *Musée* again this morning—talking with another man. Unfortunately, that guy had his back to me, and by the time I could work my way through the crowds and across the street, to come at them from the other direction, they had all gone inside. They must still be in there—unless they left by a back door. I'll go back and watch for a while after we split up here."

"Did you get some idea of what the third man looked like?" Maggie asked, her heart thumping. "Is there some way we might recognize him if we saw him? You know—a walk? Hunched shoulders? Maybe he was bowlegged?"

Simon squinted his eyes, concentrating. "He was the tallest of the three—you-know-who being the shortest. No special walk that I could detect in three steps. Thin. Gray business suit— very stylish. Black hair as neat as my Aunt Lucy's Sunday table-cloth. At least, from the back." Simon unsquinted his eyes. "Afraid that's all I can say."

Maggie tapped the sides of her cheeks in frustration at the appearance of another partial, not very helpful clue, but Jean-Louis saw it differently.

"It is good," he said. "The thieves are coming into one place— as vultures around a dead body."

"Oooh, could you put that another way?" Maggie wrung her hands. "I'm getting scared. After not seeing Madame DuBois for ages," she told Simon, "we've seen her twice since yesterday. Last evening she stayed in the park next door for the longest time—all rigged up in a maroon dress and shawl. This morning she got to the church even before Jean-Louis and I met in the courtyard at six, and she didn't leave until after ten."

"At this time, she wore a brown dress and a shawl of a lighter color," Jean-Louis added, rubbing his leg in short spurts of mo-tion that told Maggie his excitement was growing. "We have still never seen her with Gérard. Maybe they are both criminals and she is double-crossing him?"

"Dunno." Simon shrugged. "You two probably shouldn't risk being seen by Gérard around these parts, so I'll go back to the café and hang out a little longer—see if any of your suspects come out of the *Musée*. After that, my sketchbook and I are off to continue making my fortune."

"That is all right," Jean-Louis said. "Maggie and I must hurry to pass through much celebrating on the way back to the convent."

"Have to get there in time to help Sr. Clare with a special Bastille Day supper," Maggie explained. "But we can meet again.

How about tomorrow afternoon—before we have to go to supper with my friend and the Sisters?"

"*Oui,* Simon. That is good?"

"Don't you two ever quit?" Simon exploded in a burst of exasperation. "Don't you realize I've given you prime time on a major holiday, and that tomorrow's Sunday?" His irritation hit and quit as fast as a slammed door, but it struck Maggie like a shot arrow. She bit her lip and tried not to do anything silly, like burst into tears.

Simon glanced at what must have been her stricken look. "Oh, what the heck," he said. "What's a holiday when there's important work to be done, right? Catch you on the quay across from Notre Dame at two o'clock tomorrow." Simon unfolded his long legs, secured his ever-present sketchpad under his arm, and slipped out of sight past a group of customers leaving the bookshop.

"If we're going to keep Sr. Clare's paintings from getting stolen, or Tara from getting sold," Maggie said, looking out at the spot where Simon had disappeared past the crowd, "we're going to have to find out an awful lot in a very short time."

✦ 16 ✦

Telltale Footprints

MAGGIE AND JEAN-LOUIS crossed back to *Ile de la Cité* with a festive crowd going in the same direction, and discovered a pantalooned fire-eater performing in front of the Cathedral. Maggie rubbed her throat gingerly, watching him swallow firebrands big enough to light a city block on a moonless night.

On the other side of the church, by the main sidewalk, she and Jean-Louis found a swinging blues/jazz band surrounded by an enthusiastic clapping-in-time audience. A team of clowns danced by, leading a growing string of participants in line dancing down the street.

All things considered, Maggie thought, she and Jean-Louis got back to the convent quicker than they might have—in time to help the Sisters carry the prepared dishes of food to the dining room.

Sr. Clare hardly seemed to notice their return, not even enough to scold them for being so late, and after everyone had passed around the cold ham and carrot salad, Maggie picked up on her aunt's mood and broke into a rapid jerky-puppet tap sequence against the front legs of her chair and the dining room carpet underneath. She grinned across the table at Jean-Louis, who tapped out an answering sequence. He had picked up on it too—Sr. Clare was HYPER!

Sure enough, three minutes later, when everyone else had barely started chewing, Sr. Clare practically leaped out of her chair. "Gérard *must* have finished making that last crate by now."

She talked faster than she had eaten. "As soon as he and I get the paintings packed into the crates and sealed, he can go home and get a good night's sleep. Fr. Francois has offered to lock up tonight for him and keep an eye on things. See you all later!" She stuffed her napkin into its ring, tossed it onto the sideboard of the china cabinet, and started out of the room.

"Oops!" She stopped long enough to say, "Thanks for getting all the paper work in order, Thérèse—it's splendid. And thanks for helping with supper, Germaine. Will you two kids do the dishes?" She smiled apologetically at everyone in general. "I really must run."

"It will be a good thing for my digestive system if she doesn't do too many overseas exhibits," Sr. Thérèse said dryly after Sr. Clare was gone. The glamorous nun sat back in her chair, her arms folded across her presumably aching stomach.

Sr. Germaine winked at Maggie and Jean-Louis, and got up to clear the table.

A couple trips of helping carry dishes to the kitchen gave Maggie the first quiet moments she'd had since seeing Simon that afternoon. Thoughts of paintings, thefts and the need to find more clues flooded back into her mind.

"Sr. Clare's pretty excited all right," she said when she and Jean-Louis were alone in the kitchen doing dishes, "but my nerves are jangly. Who do you think the tall guy with Gérard and the guard was? Where do you think he went after Simon saw him?" Maggie didn't wait for an answer. "When we came into the presbytery this afternoon, I was in too much of a hurry to think of it at the time, but I had the eeriest feeling that we were being watched."

"I too felt this." Jean-Louis pulled a glass out of the rinse basin and watched the water drip from it. "I heard Gérard hammering in the working room when we arrived, so it could not have been him, do you think?"

"I'm beginning to think there are more suspects around us than hornets around a nest. Oh, by the way, when we were clearing the table, Sr. Germaine said she wants to come to the fireworks with us tonight. That's okay, isn't it? The other two aren't interested."

"Magnificent." Jean-Louis twisted his dishtowel into a whip and snapped it at a spider on the windowsill. Luckily for the spider, he missed. "I am wondering," he said, letting his towel go limp, "if something might happen tonight—perhaps during the fireworks."

"Yeah, I know what you mean. Like, somebody sneaking in to steal one of Sr. Clare's paintings while everybody's attention is diverted. Hey, I've got it!" Maggie clapped her hands in the dishwater, sending soapsuds billowing out of the sink. "We'll set a trap!"

At eleven o'clock that night, while Jean-Louis waited with Sr. Germaine in the courtyard, Maggie, who pretended she had to go upstairs for something she had forgotten, sprinkled a good, but almost invisible layer of baby powder around the locked workroom door and all the way down that side of the hall to the church archway.

Stowing the nearly empty container in an unused cupboard of the parish kitchen, she joined Jean-Louis and Sr. Germaine in the courtyard. "Ready," she said, directing one meaning to the unsuspecting nun and another to Jean-Louis. "Sr. Clare says to have a nice time and to be quiet when we get home. I think Sr. Thérèse is already asleep."

"Also, I believe," Jean-Louis said innocently, "is *Père* Francois. He has checked the building an hour ago, and has said to be sure to lock the courtyard door when we leave and when we return. *Soeur* Germaine? Maggie?" With a sweeping bow, he ushered the two of them out onto the sidewalk, closed the big door, and locked it with the key Maggie knew his father had given him long ago for running errands to and from the church at odd hours.

The city was aglow with light, and the Bastille Day fireworks emblazoned the sky above in a stupendous display of color and design. Maggie loved it, and a part of her wondered if she would run into Tanya. But the biggest part of her remained focused on the presbytery floor outside Gérard's workroom. What would be there when they returned?

"I will hide in the parish kitchen for the rest of tonight," Jean-Louis whispered to Maggie under cover of the noisy fireworks. "My parents will be asleep, and I have already told them that I will enter very quietly and not wake them up. They will not miss me."

At a little after one o'clock in the morning, Maggie, Jean-Louis and Sr. Germaine returned to the convent. Inside the presbytery, at the bottom of the winding staircase, Maggie surreptitiously strained to see if there were any marks in the dusting of powder on the hallway floor. As far as she could tell, there wasn't so much as a mouse track.

"I will see you tomorrow, Maggie," Jean-Louis said with a hidden wink. *Bonne nuit, Soeur* Germaine."

Upstairs in her room, knowing that Jean-Louis was probably not going to get any sleep, Maggie felt guilty about climbing into her comfortable bed. She was probably too keyed up to sleep, either. But just in case, she set her travel alarm and tucked it under her pillow so nobody else would hear it. Then, listening to the neighborhood theater and coffee house hubbub, she lay down to rest.

The muffled ring of her alarm shot her awake. She sat up and shook her head to clear away the dregs of sleep. Five-thirty already!

Having to consider proper clothes for Sunday Mass forced Maggie to take longer than her usual five minutes to dress. But she still didn't waste any time, and at exactly five-forty, she grabbed her camera and ran downstairs.

"Maggie!" Jean-Louis stood immediately inside the presbytery door. "Look there, by the room!"

From the last stair step, Maggie looked. Even in the inadequate lighting of the big hall, she could see them. Footprints.

"Wow! Oh, wowweewillikers!" She broke into a spontaneous tap routine from the step to the floor and back onto the step. "It's incredible!" She tiptoed toward the workroom and squatted down for a closer look.

"One set, going both ways—*from* the courtyard, back to the courtyard. Who was it? Did you see?"

Jean-Louis grimaced. "I was afraid that you would ask. I fell asleep in the kitchen and did not see anyone. But I think I know. Look here."

Jean-Louis came and drew Maggie back toward the presbytery door. Halfway there, at the archway that opened into the church, he stopped. "Our suspect did not come from the courtyard. You see?"

Maggie saw. "The suspect came from inside the church! There aren't any footprints from the church to the archway, because he hadn't run into any powder yet. But it's plain as day that he went from the work room back to here."

Maggie bent over to study the evidence. Two strong footprints, followed by less and less delineated ones, led from the hallway, through the archway, into the church, and straight toward the choir stall.

Maggie shook her hands, the way a person would to shake water from them—but she was shaking away her own racing thoughts. "Do you know what this means, Jean-Louis?" she said, adjusting her camera to get photos of each set of prints in the hall and in the archway.

"Yes!"

Maggie looked up from her picture taking in time to see Jean-Louis's brown eyes light up in their hot-on-the-trail expression.

"Someone has hidden in the church," he said, "until the doors were locked in the evening and Gérard went away. Until *we* went away. We are fortunate not to have been seen sprinkling the powder! It is that person who must have also been watching us yesterday afternoon."

"Yeah. And the little size of the prints tells us who—sneaky old Madame DuBois!"

"*Mais, oui!*"

"But what the heck is she up to? We always see her *around* Gérard, but never *with* him. Wouldn't it be something if she really were double crossing him? She'd better watch out—we've got some great evidence here!" Maggie tapped the camera hanging around her neck.

"That is what I am also thinking. This afternoon, we will see if Simon has discovered more clues. But first, I must go home to change my clothes and pretend that I have been there all night. And after Mass, I must eat breakfast at home. My mother is not feeling well since yesterday, so you will meet only my father today."

"Okay, see you then."

At Mass, Maggie had a hard time settling down, but the choir sang beautifully, and she realized that *Monsieur* Gagnon must be as good a director as Jean-Louis had said he was. That didn't make her any more anxious to meet the man who seemed to treat Jean-Louis so badly, though.

"I am pleased to meet the friend of my son," *Monsieur* Gagnon said formally after Mass, his thin face still flushed from directing the choir's final hymn. Meeting Maggie's eyes for only a split second, he shook her hand with his right one and ran the fingers of his left through his hair in a futile attempt to tame the tangle of black curls so like Jean-Louis'. "We must go now. My wife is recovering from flu, and we will go home to have our meal with her. Goodbye. *Soeur* Clare. Germaine. Thérèse." He nodded briefly to each nun as he spoke her name. "Come, Jean-Louis." Without another word, he strode toward the presbytery door and went outside to the courtyard.

"Fifteen minutes until two o'clock, I will come here," Jean-Louis said to Maggie, and followed his father through the presbytery door.

"Mr. Gagnon sure doesn't waste any time being friendly," Maggie muttered, staring at the closed door.

"Remember, he blames his son's accident entirely on himself," Sr. Clare said, putting her arm around Maggie's shoulders. "He acts angry with Jean-Louis, but it's really himself he despises. I pray every day for something to break through his misery enough for him to see that it's Jean-Louis's spirit that is getting crippled because of his behavior, much more than his leg." Sr. Clare sighed, then gently turned Maggie around and guided her toward the ninety-nine steps. "What do you say we whip up some eggs and bacon?" she said as they climbed the stairs with Sr. Germaine and Sr. Thérèse.

The American-fried eggs and crisp bacon were delicious, but Maggie had trouble keeping her mind on her food. And the mealtime conversation and dishes seemed to take forever. She was relieved when it was finally time to change clothes and run downstairs to meet Jean-Louis.

"Hi," she called as soon as he entered the courtyard. "We have to be back here by four, so I can change into Sunday clothes again and be ready to go for supper. Hey, where are *your* good clothes?"

"I cannot go for supper." Jean-Louis shrugged. "I do not know if it is because my mother is still not feeling well, as my father says, or if it is because he does not wish me to be seen by an important American businessman who could ask me questions about what has happened to my leg. You see for yourself why it is hard for me to forgive him." Jean-Louis picked up a loose pebble from the cobblestone floor of the courtyard and hurled it at the crypt stairwell. The pebble clinked down the cement stairs, and stopped.

"*Mais,*" Jean Louis said, breaking the silence, "I may still go to the Left Bank with you this afternoon."

"Good. Let's go, before somebody thinks of some reason why we can't do that either."

As soon as she got to *Ile de la Cité,* Maggie started scanning the droves of tourists and churchgoers.

"It looks as though everybody in the world is here," she said, "except Simon." She watched people pour out of Notre Dame Cathedral the way they had poured away from the baggage claim area at the airport. "Where is that guy?"

"I do not know. It is two o'clock—he should be here."

"Do you think something happened to him?"

"I do not think so. But I do not understand. Perhaps he has discovered someone at the *Musée* once again, and is following him." Standing still, watching the scattering of people that came only intermittently, now, out of Notre Dame, Jean-Louis rested his weight on his strong leg and rubbed the other one methodically. "We must separate. Wait here, Maggie, to see if Simon comes. I will go to the café and to the *Musée.*"

By three-thirty, Maggie and Jean-Louis had taken turns scouting out from the Cathedral in all directions, and still no Simon.

At last Maggie said, "I have to go, Jean-Louis. Don't forget to meet me at *La Boulangerie* at eleven-thirty. Oh, rats." She wrung her hands and gave the Square a final survey. "I have this idea that if I turned around fast enough and looked at just the right spot, I'd see Simon—or someone who would know where he is. Something is happening right under our noses. I can feel it."

17

Frère Jacques to the Rescue

BY A QUARTER TO FIVE, standing near the curb outside the main entrance of the church with the Sisters, Maggie still hadn't lost the feeling of hidden action going on all around her. If only she could snatch a few minutes with Tanya alone. She could fill her in and get her to help do a little detective work somehow.

"We could have walked to the restaurant and met Richard and his daughter there," Sr. Clare said, looking out at the cars passing by them. "But he said it would be simpler to stop by for us in the limousine. That way, we'll all get there together and be able to order right away."

"This is not a civilized hour or manner in which to eat." Sr. Thérèse pursed her lips in an almost Tanya-like pout.

Sr. Germaine kept her silence, whether from lack of understanding or simply not wanting to get involved in the grumbling, Maggie couldn't tell.

A long black car pulled up to the curb, stopping any further talk, and a uniformed chauffer emerged from the driver's seat. He came around to open the back door, and motioned for the Sisters and Maggie to enter.

The last one in, Maggie found herself in the middle of introductions.

"Good evening, Sr. Clare," Tanya was saying. "Maggie has told me so much about you." Sounding politely adult, and dressed in a white linen suit with a flared skirt, Tanya sat in the limousine as though in a royal blue velvet throne. She shook Maggie's aunt's hand. "Hi, Maggie." Dropping the adult, Tanya wiggled her eyebrows, Groucho Marx style, and Maggie laughed.

"Hi, Tanya. Nice wheels." She looked around. "Where's your dad?"

"He's with *Monsieur* Brière, the fabric designer we met with yesterday," Tanya said, taking on an affected air again. "He said he'll meet us at the restaurant as soon as possible, and I'm to order something good for him."

At the restaurant, Maggie smothered her irritation at Tanya's airs by trying to match them. She managed to act like a model of sophistication when being seated by the waiter and when scanning the menu, but with Tanya's order she lost all ground.

"Rooster!" she exclaimed after the waiter left. "How could you? Your own father!"

"It's a delicacy," Tanya said haughtily. "Isn't it, Sisters?"

Sr. Clare nodded, and Sr. Thérèse said, "Of course it is." But Maggie knew neither of them had caught Tanya's wicked grin.

A plate of hors d'oeuvres came very quickly, and Maggie discovered how hungry she was. She ate the crackers and cheese with enthusiasm and wondered what Jean-Louis and his parents were eating for their Sunday supper.

The waiter cleared all their used plates away and waited discreetly in the background for Mr. Becker to arrive, before serving the main course.

At last, Maggie saw Tanya's father, tall, handsome and harried, rush into the restaurant and up the stairs to the table by the window where the rest of them sat waiting. His entrance triggered something in the back of Maggie's mind, but before she could grasp what it was, it was gone.

Seated in his place, Mr. Becker hurried distractedly through introductions, and spent the rest of the meal in an intense one-on-one conversation with Sr. Clare. Sr. Thérèse listened attentively and sometimes added a sentence or two about forms and regulations for shipping things overseas.

Tanya rolled her eyes and, breaking from her sophisticated princess role, yawned widely.

"We can teach you some more English, Sr. Germaine," Maggie suggested.

In what seemed only a few moments, Maggie and Tanya taught the little nun several useful phrases, such as "That is truly awesome," "T'sup," and "'Give me a home where the buffalo roam.'" Plus a few more mundane ones like "May I use the telephone?" and "Thank you for the delicious meal."

Shoot, Maggie thought, when Tanya's father beckoned to the waiter for the bill, there went her chance to talk to Tanya alone.

The limousine ride didn't offer any better opportunities for private conversation. The adults were mostly quiet, and the trip to the convent only took a few minutes.

"Thank you for the delicious meal," Sr. Germaine said with a French accent that Maggie would have liked to have for her own. The small nun shook Mr. Becker's hand and slipped out of the car past the chauffeur, who had come around to open the door. Sr. Thérèse and Sr. Clare followed Sr. Germaine. And then it was Maggie's turn.

"Bye, Tanya. Have a good trip home and everything," she added quickly, remembering in time that this was supposed to be a real parting. "See you in a few weeks. Goodbye, Mr. Becker."

Tanya managed a hidden wink in Maggie's direction. "See you."

As Maggie started to get out of the limousine, Sr. Clare was saying, "Let's go around the block and through the park. It's cooler now, and it'll be nice to be outside for a few minutes." She and the other two Sisters started down the sidewalk.

Maggie stepped back from the limo to let the driver close the car door. In one smooth movement of stern formality, he closed the door and returned to his side of the car.

"Bye, Tanya," Maggie called through the dark passenger window. She waved, and, intending to catch up with the Sisters, turned away from the curb—directly into the path of an old woman in a big hurry.

"Yipes!" Maggie jumped back, landing hard against the limousine. Before she could catch her balance, the woman thrust something into her hand and scuttled across the street.

Dazed, Maggie pushed herself away from the car. "Sorry," she said toward the steel-gray limousine window.

The window rolled down, and Tanya poked her head out. "You okay?"

"Yeah, thanks. Go ahead."

The car pulled away from the curb and out of sight before the window was even halfway rolled back up.

The edges of the folded paper pressed into Maggie's closed hand. Still dazed, she looked to see if the Sisters had noticed what had happened. Apparently not. Already at the gate, they opened it and started across the park. Maggie followed silently.

"Coming, Maggie?" Sr. Clare called from the other side of the park. She and the other nuns stood at the far gate, near the church courtyard.

"Not yet," Maggie said, sitting on one of the park benches. "I'd like to stay out here a little while, if it's okay."

"Sure. Don't stay too long, though. We want to close up early and get a good night's sleep. See you when you come up."

Maggie curled her hand around the mysterious paper and left her bench to walk to the courtyard. She wanted to be close to home when she read whatever message this turned out to be. She had known from the first instant, of course, that the woman had been Madame DuBois. But what was the hit-and-run all about?

The courtyard and church seemed quiet, but judging by the previous day, that didn't necessarily mean that nobody was around. Maggie sat on the top of the three presbytery steps and kept alert as she thought things over. It must be around eight o'clock now—still plenty light out. But it wouldn't be in three hours, when she had to sneak out of the convent and work her way toward the *boulangerie,* where Jean-Louis would meet her.

Maggie brought her hand to her mouth, intending to gnaw on a fingernail, and wondered for a second what in the world a piece of paper was doing in her hand.

"Oh, yeah, Madame DuBois." She opened the paper slowly, one fold at a time, until what she held was a full notebook-sized sheet filled with a scrawled handwriting worse only than her own.

Having to concentrate on deciphering the writing eased some
of the fear of what she was about to read.

> *"Sorry I was late this afternoon. Made lots of money
> sketching portraits at Montmartre and forgot about the
> time."*

"Simon!" Maggie exclaimed, and bent to read the rest of his
scribbled message.

> *"Lots happening. Important sketch to show you.
> Will meet you and Jean-Louis tonight at 11:30 near
> Notre Dame, Shakespeare and Company or the hotel.
> Most important of all—the bearer of this note is trust-
> worthy."*

"If only I could call Jean-Louis," Maggie murmured. "But I
don't dare. It would be too easy for someone to overhear us."
She folded Simon's note and put it into the pocket of her skirt
where it would be safe.

"Come here, *Frère* Jacques," she said, picking up the cat that
had wandered over to the presbytery steps from a spot under a
stained glass window of the church. He must have been soaking
up the last rays of the evening sun.

"What are we going to do, old friend?" she crooned. "Jean-
Louis said to try and get a nap before we head out again, but
how can I possibly sleep?"

She couldn't. Couldn't read, either. Upstairs in her room, at
nine o'clock, she changed from her Sunday skirt to a pair of
white capris and sat fully dressed on top of her quilt, thumping
her heels softly against the side of the bed. She listened to the
Sisters leave the little chapel across from her room after praying
Compline—night prayer.

"I'll introduce Richard Becker to Gérard tomorrow morning," Sr. Clare was saying as the three nuns passed by Maggie's
door, "at the airport. After all the Paris buying trips for his
boutique, Richard still doesn't speak any more French than a
first-day language student, and, of course, Gérard doesn't speak
English. I'll have to do all the translating."

"I'll take care of things here at the house," Sr. Thérèse said,
"and Germaine will be doing the meals, so you won't have to
worry about anything other than getting your paintings safely

on their way and then coming back and collapsing for a few hours."

"Thanks, Thérèse. Now we'd all better get some sleep. Four-thirty tomorrow morning is going to come soon enough. Is Maggie in?" A brief second elapsed, and a soft knock sounded at Maggie's door. "Anybody home?"

Maggie had already started toward the door. She opened it, and nodded. "Yep, I'm kind of tired too." She returned her aunt's good night hug.

"You okay about not going to the airport in the morning, Maggie? I know it would be nice for you to see Tanya again, but it will be so hectic at that point. Another dynamic would be too much."

"It's okay, honest. It would only be for a second, anyway."

"You're a dear. Goodnight, now. I'll see you tomorrow."

After Maggie closed her door and returned to sit on her bed again, she waited for a long time after the sounds of bedtime rustlings stopped and quiet descended on the convent. The need for sleep pushed her eyelids downward, but she didn't dare give in now.

Ten forty-five. Trying not to think of what lay ahead, Maggie let another agonizing fifteen minutes go by. Finally, at eleven o'clock, she couldn't wait any longer. She got up from her bed and picked up her small backpack with its contents of a sweater, comb and Tanya's book from Shakespeare and Company. Holding the bag close to her with one arm, she tiptoed past the Sisters' bedrooms and out into the big hall. The regular winding staircase beckoned. Surely it would be okay to go this way. The building felt still and quiet. The big stairs would be so much easier. No slimy stone steps. No being trapped between walls. Yeah, this was much better than the secret stairs.

Instead of crossing the landing to the kitchen apartment, Maggie took the first step downward. She waited a second, and took another. Enough city light shone through the little window above the landing to guide her way. She lifted her foot to take another step down—and froze.

Somewhere on the first floor, a door shut softly. A rapid, low-voiced conversation rose up through the hollow corridor. One of the voices was Gérard's. Maggie couldn't mistake his familiar grumbling. Something was strange about it, though. What was it? She could only catch a word here and there. English words. Sr. Clare had said Gérard didn't speak English. So, who could it be down there, if it wasn't Gérard? There was something weird about the other voice, too. Something familiar.

Footsteps pattered almost soundlessly through the first floor hall, and the tops of two heads passed by twenty feet below Maggie.

Already plastered against the wall, she stopped breathing. Two men. One short and thin, with a jerky walk—it *was* Gérard!

The other man—tall, straight as an army colonel—who could he be? Maggie knew she should know him. She watched the tops of their heads disappear as they passed along the hall and out of her view. Suddenly, the back of the tall man's head, with its clean-lined haircut, clicked a door open in Maggie's memory. "Black hair as neat as Aunt Lucy's tablecloth." Simon's description of the third man he had seen with Gérard and the museum guard came back to her.

Okay, so that was it. Maggie should be satisfied. But she wasn't. She should recognize that man—even from the back. The way he moved and talked . . .

Oh! Maggie clasped her hand over her mouth to keep from crying out. Mr. Becker! But it couldn't be! Shivering with more than the cold, she edged away from the wall.

Afraid to move very far, and working hard at convincing herself she was wrong about the man with Gérard, Maggie waited until she heard the presbytery door open and close. It clicked so quietly she had to strain to hear it. After waiting another full minute, to be sure the men were gone, she made herself retreat up the two steps she had come down and unlock the door to the Sisters' kitchen apartment. Once inside, she ran to the pantry, grabbed the flashlight from the phone table, and walked to the secret door. Her hand trembling, she pulled the door open.

"Eeuw, stinko!" She stepped inside before she could chicken out. Remembering the door, she reached back to close it. "I must be totally crazy," she muttered, following the flashlight beam down the spiraling cement steps. "Inside a bell tower in Paris, France, thinking I just saw my own friend's father with a crook." Her mind reeled, and she pushed all thought away. Concentrate on one thing at a time, she told herself sternly.

"Rats. Should have put my sweater on. Oh, well . . ." Maggie tried not to think of all the creepy, crawly things she might run into in the dark as she continued circling her way downward. With every step, she wanted more and more to run back upstairs and snuggle into her warm, safe bed. The bottom hadn't been this far away the day she and Jean-Louis had found the secret stairs.

At last, Maggie made it to the door at the bottom. She eased the latch up, swung the door open, and peeked into the church. Dark. Quiet. Empty. She crept across the stone floor, keeping her eye on pillars she might have to duck behind.

"The principle door to the church is locked tightly at night," Jean-Louis had warned her. "You cannot leave that way. You must go through the courtyard. Be careful not to run into, how does Simon say, you-know-who."

Yeah, Maggie thought, Gérard, and whoever was with him.

She edged from the secret stairwell to the archway that led to the church foyer and the presbytery door that opened to the courtyard. She put her ear to the door. Not a sound. Inching the heavy door open, she peeked through the crack. Yep, there was Gérard across the courtyard and to her left, near the outer wall door. In the dark, his Charlie-Chaplin figure blended in with the high stone wall that separated the courtyard from the park next door. All Maggie could see clearly was the red glow of his lit cigarette. She sensed, more than saw, that the other man was still with him.

Yes, someone—not Gérard—was opening the courtyard door now. By the distant light of a street lamp, Maggie could see that it was the other man who had been inside the presbytery. He turned from the door to say something to Gérard. Maggie caught sight of his profile—and gasped. It *was* Tanya's father!

She gripped the handle of the presbytery as if holding it would also hold her together. She should have known all along, but no part of her had been able to believe the truth. It had taken this extra nudge to bring it to the surface. Dizziness engulfed Maggie, and she leaned her forehead against the door, trying to think straight. All those attempts to get rid of Bartholomew—hinting that her stepfather was a thief. All smoke screens. It was Mr. Becker who was the thief! He and Gérard—and who else? That museum guard? Someone else in a new sketch of Simon's? Who could tell about Madame DuBois now? Whoever they were, and however many, they had all probably stolen those earlier missing paintings—including the Dumolin—and now they were plotting together to steal one of Sr. Clare's. And probably try to pin it all on Bartholomew. The no-good rats! Maggie had to get to Jean-Louis and warn him. And the two of them had to get to Notre Dame and the Left Bank in time to look for Simon before they went to the hotel. Mr. Becker had left as soon as he had delivered whatever parting words he'd had for Gérard. But the little night watchman didn't look about to budge from his position near the wall door.

"Ah, piece of *gateau*," Maggie murmured. "The oldest trick in the book—any book." She cracked open the presbytery door a little farther and bent down to pick up a loose pebble from the edge of the top cement step. She threw the pebble across the courtyard toward the sunken crypt stairs.

When the pebble hit the cobblestone floor of the courtyard, Gérard swung his head toward the sound. He snapped to attention and flicked his cigarette out, dousing the red glow of his sharp features into a single black silhouette.

"*Qui-est-là?*" His barked question brought only silence, and Gérard took two hunched steps toward the crypt stairs.

Maggie slipped all the way out the door hoping against hope that the night watchman would continue toward the crypt but terrified that he wouldn't. She kept her eyes glued on him as she sneaked soundlessly along the presbytery wall, circling toward the courtyard door.

Her heart stopped when Gérard stopped. His flashlight shining, he started to turn back to his post at the courtyard door. In a split second, the light would land on Maggie. She was done for!

A scrabbling noise on the crypt steps, followed by a sharp click, stopped Gérard mid-turn. The bright ray of his flashlight beam swerved back toward the crypt, and he took a step in that direction.

Safely outside the beam of light, Maggie found another pebble and tossed it toward the sunken stairs. Gérard stopped abruptly when the stone plinked ahead of him, then moved again, in a crouch, toward the crypt.

Behind him, Maggie slipped quietly along the presbytery wall, made the turn at the housekeeper's wall, and went along it toward the courtyard door while Gérard continued to move away from her, still creeping toward the crypt. He shone his light down the stairwell.

"Shah!" he snorted. *"C'est toi, petit coquin!"*

Maggie froze mid-step behind Gérard. He wasn't even looking in her direction—he couldn't have caught her!

A high-pitched meow told Maggie what had happened. *Frère* Jacques popped out of the crypt stairwell and darted toward the presbytery steps, Gérard at his heels.

Maggie grabbed her chance, and made a run for it to the courtyard door.

"Remind me to buy you the best can of tuna in town, you beautiful cat," she said silently as she shoved the heavy door open and leaped outside the courtyard to the sidewalk. It took all the will power she had to close the door quietly behind her before taking off like a chased fox through the lamp-lit back streets of Paris, her pack bouncing against her back as she ran.

18

Midnight Banquet

MAGGIE RAN DOWN the sidewalk into a far different world from the one she had experienced the night before. The jovial crowds of Bastille Day had disintegrated into one or two pedestrians wandering through a hollow gray world of cement. The innocent stone buildings of daylight had given way to flat-faced night giants with hundreds of square black eyes staring blankly at Maggie from both sides of the street. Only sporadic conversation spurted out of the neighborhood coffeehouses. And, to top it all off, a pin-pricking mist broke out, fuzzing the meager light from the street lamps and plastering Maggie's hair to her head as she ran.

"You'd better be there, Jean-Louis," she panted.

By the middle of the third block, she was soaked. Not much farther, though. One short block to the right. She rounded the corner at top speed.

"What the . . .!" Maggie skidded to a stop. The whole block looked like an end-of-the-world sci-fi movie. No vegetable stand or flower shop. No fish market. Only boarded walls, iron grates, and a blank window where the *boulangerie* should have been.

"This can't be real. No way. Everything is just fine here." Maggie brushed her hand across her dripping bangs. "Mr. Becker's asleep at his hotel. Gérard's in the crypt, cleaning up after the little kids and grousing about having to do it. The *boulangerie* is right here where it should be. Yep, everything's just. . ."

144

Maggie shrugged off her pack and dropped it to the wet sidewalk. Goose bumps tingling on her arms, she squatted down to open her pack and pull out her sweater. All the time she re-zipped her pack and stood to put on her sweater, she kept wondering, where's Jean-Louis? She choked back the lump in her throat. What if she ran into Mr. Becker?

"Maggie—*ici!* I am here!"

Maggie caught her breath. The rain-blurred form of a capped mushroom ran toward her with a familiar gait.

"Jean-Louis! I was afraid you were . . . an umbrella! Why wasn't I that smart? Where have you been? Wait 'til you hear what I have to tell you. What kind of disaster hit this block?"

"Oh, poor Maggie." Jean-Louis rolled to a stop, picked up her backpack, and started her off in the direction from which he had come.

"Many shops fold up at night," he explained as they walked. "Their owners do what you call, live in a suitcase. They pack their merchandise and put up a protective wall for the night.

"Oh. Well, listen." Maggie blurted out the story of Simon's note and the shocking news of who the third man in Simon's sketch was while Jean-Louis guided her down one more block of the almost deserted back street.

"We are getting very near to something important," Jean-Louis exclaimed. "But I am sorry for the sake of your friend."

"Yeah, me too. She thought it was my new father who was a crook, and it looks like it's hers instead. Oh, my gasping gold-fish—Bastille Day lives on!"

The muffled hum and throb of a distant city at night erupted into a blast of noise and light as Maggie and Jean-Louis came around the corner of a tall brick building and onto the expansive sidewalk of the action-packed *Rue de Rivoli*. Maggie should have been prepared. She'd experienced the abrupt change before. But the holiday was over, and it was almost midnight, for Pete's sake. "Doesn't anybody in Paris ever sleep?"

Jean-Louis laughed. "This is a normal night in the center of Paris. The time for supper in the restaurants usually begins at nine o'clock—not like your early supper of today. Many people wait to eat until after going to the theater or a movie or something of that nature. Now is when our city comes most to life. With so many lights on, the night becomes brighter than the day. That is why Paris is called the 'City of Light.' Come." He took Maggie's hand, and together they strolled down the bright crowded avenue.

Walking so closely beside Jean-Louis, Maggie felt a strange tingling tickle her toes. She didn't know whether the tingling was because she wanted to tap dance the City of Light, or if it was because her hand felt so right in Jean-Louis'. In spite of the drizzle, she grew warm all over, and for several moments, she forgot to watch for trouble or keep an eye out for Simon.

She and Jean-Louis crossed the two bridges that took them past *Ile St. Louis* to *Ile de la Cité*. Nearing Notre Dame Cathedral, they slowed down and looked carefully through the late-night gatherings of tourists and other groups.

"Simon is not here," Jean-Louis said at last.

"Shall we call the police?"

"Oui." Jean-Louis started to walk past Notre Dame and toward the bridge to the Left Bank. "As soon as we find Simon and hear what he has discovered."

"What if we don't find him?" Maggie's eyes burned from looking so hard behind every person she saw. "Maybe he's holed up under a roof ledge somewhere, still drawing some . . . hey, look down there, at the end of the quay. Somebody's sketching under an umbrella. Who else but Simon would be that dingy to . . ." Maggie was already running across the bridge and down the stairs to the long wharf, Jean-Louis beside her, still holding her hand. They stopped short.

"A girl," Maggie groaned. As one, she and Jean-Louis climbed up the steps and walked down the block toward Shakespeare and Company.

The bookshop looked as deserted as the block around the *boulangerie* had. A few scattered lights shone through the windows of the various floors, but there wasn't a soul in sight.

"They are closed," Jean-Louis said needlessly. The umbrella tipped in his hand, sending a trickle of water onto Maggie's head. Hardly aware of what she was doing, she let go of Jean-Louis' hand to brush the water out of her hair and away from her eyes.

"He'll be at the hotel," she said as doubtfully as she felt.

She and Jean-Louis walked slowly past *Musée Millénaire Nouveau* and dared to peek inside the café across the street from it. No Simon.

"It is midnight," Jean-Louis said. "Your friend will be waiting for us."

"Yeah, and, hopefully, Simon too. And, hopefully, *not* Mr. Becker."

In spite of being late, the closer they got to the hotel, the slower Maggie walked. "I know I've been blabbing all along about getting Tanya to help us with our detective work, but that idea's goners now. I can't tell her we think her father might be a crook. She rebels against him a lot, all right, but that's just it. Her whole world revolves around him. Everything she thinks, everything she says is related to him. Her life would be emptier than that closed bookshop without him in it. She would lose the main reason for her existence. What can we do?"

"I do not know." Jean-Louis pointed to an imposing gray-stone building on the far side of the street, took Maggie's hand again, and led her, dodging traffic, across the street. "It is good that she, too, does not want to be seen by him tonight."

"Yeah, you're right." Maggie looked up and down the block. "No Simon anywhere here either."

She turned her attention to the wide, oak-framed double glass doors of *Hotel La Fleur*. Graceful columns of ivy wound their way upward, clinging to the stone on either side of the doors. Pastel stained glass flowers decorated the rectangular windows set into the wall to the right of the doors. Maggie pulled her long braid around front to try and subdue the rain-soaked frizzy ends.

"You look very fine, Maggie. Come."

Maggie was glad for the mist that hid her pink cheeks as Jean-Louis greeted the doorman and escorted her into the hotel lobby.

"Maggie!" If it hadn't been for her friend's voice, Maggie wouldn't have recognized Tanya. Dressed in a crimson floor-length jumper that showed off her long black hair, done up in ringlets on top of her head, she looked every bit the belle that belonged in this chandelier and plush-carpet world.

Her eye on Jean-Louis, Tanya hugged Maggie. "Hi, again!" She let go of Maggie and turned to Jean-Louis. *"Bonjour,* Jean-Louis. *Comment allez-vous?"* The fingernails on the hand she offered Jean-Louis glowed the same crimson as her jumper.

Maggie fiddled with the cuffs of her sodden royal blue silk blouse and tried to smooth the wrinkles in her white capris. From which oldie but goodie movie had Tanya pulled her French greeting? Clever move. It looked as though it had worked too. One glance at Jean-Louis revealed that he appeared to have fallen under her friend's spell as readily as every other boy always seemed to. The feeling of being lost and forsaken in a strange and unknown world fell over Maggie again, the way it had at the airport.

"Here, I'll stick your pack behind the reception desk. Geneviève, the hostess, won't mind." Tanya snatched the dripping backpack from Jean-Louis and ran behind the desk with it before Maggie could stop her.

Oh, well, Maggie thought. I can get Tanya's book later. "Could you put this behind there too?" She tossed her soggy sweater to Tanya.

"Have you always lived in Paris, Jean-Louis?" Tanya slipped between him and Maggie and took each one by the arm, drawing them toward the glassed-in restaurant. "Let's have an all-out bash on my dad's tab."

Maggie grimaced inwardly. It would be awful if something happened to crush Tanya's cocky, rebel spirit.

"We're having our party in the smaller restaurant," Tanya said. "More intimate. How do you like it?" As at home in this luxurious hotel as Maggie was on a mountain bike, Tanya slid onto the chair the waiter held out for her at a table that was located in a corner where two glass walls met. One wall separated the restaurant from the lobby. The other formed one side of an indoor arboretum filled with exotic-looking plants and flowers.

"We'd like a few minutes before ordering, please," Tanya told the waiter after he had seated Maggie.

The waiter obligingly distributed the leather-bound menus, inclined his head to acknowledge her request, and left.

"Willikers," Maggie said softly. Like all the other tables in the room, theirs was round, set with crystal, pale-blue china and gold cutlery on a white tablecloth that draped to within an inch of the lavender-blue carpet. All the tables in the room had small flower arrangements in the center, but this one had a huge pink-orchid arrangement decorating the center and, beside it, a gold-edged card that read, *"Bon Fête,* Maggie."

"It's stupendous. Oh, Tanya, thanks!" Not knowing what else to say, Maggie picked up the card, touched the embossed gold letter, and put it down again.

"Great place for a party, huh?" Tanya held an empty wine glass aloft. "We can celebrate all night, while Dad's asleep in his room, never knowing he's getting poorer by the minute!"

Maggie knew this was her cue to laugh at Tanya's bold reck-lessness, but she couldn't do it. "Um, Tanya, I think your dad's awake—maybe. I think I saw him on the way here. I'm not sure." Maggie squirmed in her chair.

"Awake? At this hour?" Tanya wrinkled her nose. "I bet you just saw somebody who looked like him." She broke into a grin. "If it *was* my dad, dodging him will add zip to this little. . ."

The waiter reappeared beside their table. *"Mesdemoiselles et Monsieur?"*

"A bottle of champagne, please." A ringlet of Tanya's raven hair slid loose and dipped over one eye when she looked up and batted her eyelashes at the waiter.

Maggie bit her lip to keep from giggling.

The waiter frowned, but after a quick conversation with Jean-Louis in French, he left and came back with a bottle that looked like champagne, but which Jean-Louis said was sparkling grape juice. With a flourish, the waiter filled everyone's glass, put the open bottle in a bucket of ice in a wooden stand beside the table, and went away again.

"A toast," Jean-Louis said, lifting his glass in salute, "to the birthday girl! That is a proper expression, yes? I learned it in an American book." He clinked glasses with Tanya, and they drank to Maggie.

"To our first midnight party together," she said, and drank too.

"Oh, oh, I better not forget these." Tanya pulled two enve-lopes from a little black-leather purse Maggie hadn't noticed before and put them on Maggie's plate. "I promised your mom I'd get these to you."

Maggie stared at the envelopes—so white on her blue plate. Only now did she realize a hidden fear that she hadn't let surface before. Her mother and Bartholomew hadn't forgotten her birthday. She slid her finger under the sealed flap of the top envelope. When she pulled out the card, a Polaroid print fell from the envelope too. She picked it up, turned it over, and saw the likeness of her mom, standing like a showcase model and pointing with both hands to a shiny new platinum-green bike.

Like Mighty Mammoth, the bike in the photo was a Schwinn, but any resemblance between the two instruments of transportation ended there. The one her mom pointed to in the photo was a streamlined, sturdy-looking mountain bike. The real thing. Maggie pulled her eyes away from the gleaming beauty and passed the photo to Jean-Louis. He whistled appreciatively and handed it on to Tanya.

"Oh, Maggie, your mom is so far out!" A wistful note crept into Tanya's voice. "What's in the other card? Think it'll be from that no-good, I mean, from Bartholomew?"

"He's not no-good, I keep telling you!" Maggie winced at her own defiance. She had never spoken to Tanya like that before.

Tanya's eyebrows shot up, but she recovered quickly. "Okay, okay, so what's in your new dad's envelope?"

Maggie tore it open, read the card, looked at the enclosed photo, and laughed. "Oh, good grief!" She handed the print to Jean-Louis.

"My new dad. Doesn't he look like Sr. Clare? The card is a gift certificate for one lumberjack pizza—that's what he's holding in the picture. He's going to make the pizza for me on August fourth, the day I'm supposed to return to Welcome. Hey, wait." Maggie brushed away the tears that had sprung into her eyes. "There's a gift for you, too, Tanya. And I want my sweater back. These clothes are still wet, and it's cold in here." Maggie slipped out of her chair.

"Careful, Maggie. If my dad's really up, and he sees you, I'll be grounded for the rest of the summer!" Tanya laughed. "That would give me some new challenges to conquer!"

"I'll be careful," Maggie promised, and walked away from the table. At the restaurant doorway, she scanned the lobby. Clear sailing. She turned, gave the others the thumbs up, and ran to the reception desk. If Tanya knew what might really be at stake here . . .

Maggie ducked behind the desk, picked up her sweater, threw it over her arm, and squatted to unfasten her backpack. Out of the corner of her left eye, she saw a young woman dressed in a classy, but businesslike suit, sitting in a leather easy chair at the end of the lobby and talking with a bellhop who stood beside her. She wasn't paying a bit of attention to the desk. Probably Geneviève, the hostess.

The main door, to Maggie's right, opened. Dreading what she would see, she glanced that way. Her heart skipped a beat. Two men walked into the hotel. One—Mr. Becker. The other —the hard-faced guard in Simon's sketch.

Maggie willed herself to grow smaller. She scrunched close to the inside of the overhang on the high desk. She could tell by their voices that the men were coming toward the desk. If Geneviève got up and found Maggie, and the men saw her . . .

Maggie could see Geneviève's feet and the edge of the easy chair. Oh, no, the receptionist was standing up. She was moving. Maggie felt sick. Wait. The feet stopped. Geneviève sat back down. She must have recognized Mr. Becker and realized she wouldn't have to come to the desk. Maggie's cramped knees nearly buckled.

Mr. Becker and his companion now stood directly in front of the reception desk. Maggie held her breath. The other man said in fluent, but strongly accented English, "The items are in place. Gérard telephoned just before you arrived at my place."

"Good. He was almost finished when I saw him an hour ago." That was Mr. Becker talking now. "It's impossible to tell from the outside that there's anything extra in the crates. As for any screening of the crates—André should be getting our security guards and customs officials in place right about now. When Gérard gets the crates there for the flight, our people will send them straight through. At the American end, Lester will meet me with a van. We'll load up the crates, I'll go directly to the gallery in my own car, and he'll stop en route at a spot where the buyer will meet him and the transaction will take place. The nun's paintings will reach their destination, and that ridiculous exhibit will take place right on schedule—nothing missing, nobody the wiser. Everything is going exactly as planned."

Scrunched behind the desk, Maggie felt her body go numb. That rat, Mr. Becker, *was* a crook! She fought to keep her emotions in check well enough to listen clearly. The men were talking again.

"There is one problem," the museum guard said in a tone that sent a chill down Maggie's spine. "It's a big one, *Monsieur* Becker, and we will have to do something about it immediately." The guard's voice rose in excitement, but a "shush," from Mr. Becker brought it back down again.

"When Gérard phoned me," the guard said softly but still excitedly, "he said he was putting the last painting—the Dumolin—into the crate when the nun walked into the room! It was so late, he should have had no trouble at that hour, and he had not locked the door. She came to look for the American girl—the daughter of her brother. The girl's mother forgot—how does one forget such things—the difference in time, and called to give birthday greetings to the child. After the call, the nun went to put a note under the girl's door. She saw that the door was open and there was nobody inside, so she went to look for her. It was when she finished telling Gérard this that she saw the Dumolin. He knew by her face that she recognized it."

A terrible silence followed the man's words, and Maggie wanted to kick herself. How could she have forgotten to close that dumb bedroom door?

"Maggie wasn't in her room?" Mr. Becker's voice tightened with anger. "That means my daughter might not be asleep like she should be either. She must have talked Maggie into some kind of mischief. I knew I shouldn't have let her come." Mr. Becker stopped his own rising voice. "I thought the more ordinary this trip looked," he said much more quietly, "the better it would be. Wait until I get my hands on that girl . . ."

Mr. Becker's words changed from angry pellets to calm splinters. "Yes, we'll have to do something with the nun—now."

"Do not worry, *Monsieur* Becker. Gérard has gagged her and tied her up in the crypt at the church. He said that no one will go near that place until the children's hour tomorrow evening.

It is unfortunate that he had to do this, but now he waits to receive your order of what to do."

Another pause. Maggie couldn't have breathed if she had wanted to.

"Maggie and my daughter are probably running amuck in the city somewhere," Mr. Becker said next. "Well, they'll both pay for their fun this time. Call Gérard when you leave here and tell him I'm coming to see him. Tell him not to do anything with the nun before I get there. I want to talk to that artistic traitor."

Sick with shock, Maggie reached to steady herself on the shelf under the counter. Her hand hit a coffee cup on the shelf, and, in grueling slow motion, the cup flipped into the air, arced, and dropped to the parquet floor—shattering in every direction.

For a split second after the last shard fell, the only sound in the lobby was the lazily whirring ceiling fan high above the desk.

Maggie leaped up and ran for the hotel door. Focused entirely on escape, she felt more than saw the stunned looks on the faces of the other diners in the restaurant and the running figures of Jean-Louis and Tanya on the other side of the glass wall, heading for the door that would bring them into the lobby. The two crooks, hot on her heels, would reach her first, and she knew it.

It took a lifetime to cover the few yards between the desk and the hotel entrance, but Maggie did it. Running hard, she reached out with one hand. Only two more inches and she would be able to swing the door open and be outside where she could find a place to hide. Her fingers touched the door handle.

Suddenly her whole body jerked backwards, the sweater she hadn't realized she still had in her other hand pulled taut. She let go of the sweater and plunged outside.

"Stop!"

In the confusion that followed, Maggie only knew that Jean-Louis appeared beside her, first upright, then falling. As he fell, he shot out his strong leg and tripped the guard, who, at the same time, caught Maggie's arm. She almost went down with him, but pulled away and stumbled free.

"Stop, Dad, stop! I can explain! Let him go!"

Glancing frantically over her shoulder, Maggie saw Tanya grab her father and hang on, but Mr. Becker still held Jean-Louis pinned to the sidewalk. The guard was stumbling to his feet.

Maggie ached to go back and try to help free Jean-Louis, but aware that she couldn't, and knowing she had to get to Sr. Clare, she kept running. Too late, she realized she was heading straight into a part of the city she had never seen before. There was no way she could correct her error. The museum guard plodded noisily after her.

Maggie tore around the nearest corner, raced down the block, turned right, and kept running. She ran alongside the Seine until she saw a bridge. Without a second's hesitation, she raced across it, bouncing off a group of startled merry-makers. She ran for two blocks, and approached another bridge. Maggie strained toward it. More startled crowds. More streets beyond. All of them too exposed. And bright. She had to get out of the open.

In the relentless drizzle, she darted across a wide boulevard, dodging cars and ignoring the blasts of their horns. On the other side of the street, she fought down the panic welling up in her throat. Where was she? A quick look back told her the guard was only a block behind, still pounding after her.

Maggie headed across a narrower street than the one she had just crossed, and ran this way, that way, and another way along blocks that defied right angles and provided a maze in which she might be able to lose her pursuer.

The drizzle let up, but a light mist still filled the air, and Maggie swiped the moisture from her face so she could see where she was going. She had left the broad avenues behind, and, for the second time in two hours, found herself running through the shadowed back streets of Paris, this time with Mr. Becker's last words ringing in her ears.

"Catch her, Claude, and bring her to me!"

The stitch in Maggie's side tightened with every slap of her sandals against the wet sidewalk, and at what still sounded barely a block behind, the guard pursued her. She picked up speed, pushing against the weighted sludge of fear and trying to match her brain to her rhythmically running feet.

A place to hide—that's all she needed. Maggie rounded another corner, and spotted the iron gratings of closed shops and a painted *Boulangerie* sign above a blank window. She had instinctively taken a route that had circled toward home! She had to find a place to hide fast, before dead-ending herself in her own back yard. Intent more than ever on searching for a refuge, Maggie didn't see the little old lady until she crashed into her cart.

19

Trapped!

MAGGIE FRANTICALLY untangled herself from the wheeled menace, knowing the guard—Claude—would round the corner behind her at any second. She broke free and leaped forward—right into the old woman again.

"You—what are you doing!" Maggie stumbled, and almost fell.

"Quickly!" the woman commanded in thickly accented English. She pulled a damp shawl from her own head and whipped it over Maggie's. It draped to her ankles.

"Hunch over, child, and shuffle beside me." She took Maggie firmly by the elbow and kept putting her knee into the back of Maggie's leg, causing her to flounder.

Maggie struggled to break free, but the sharp edge of her thinking blurred. Her foot kept slipping out from under her, and she couldn't muster the strength to pull away from the old woman. "What are you . . .?" she gasped.

"Shh, act drunk!" The woman, whom Maggie's muddled consciousness knew was Madame DuBois, bent Maggie's head down and kneed the back of her leg again. Maggie lurched forward.

"*Arrêtez, Mesdames! Arrêtez!*"

Maggie shivered under the long shawl. She was done for! She clutched the shawl close under her chin and stared down at the water rivulets shimmering on the sidewalk.

Madame DuBois kneed Maggie again, sending her stumbling sideways.

"Tsk, tsk." The old woman yanked on Maggie's arm, pulling her back to herself. *"Bonsoir, Monsieur. Etes-vous perdu?"* The stranger's ragged breathing broke the momentary silence. He struggled to speak, found his voice, and shouted something in French at Madame DuBois.

"Oh, oh, oh!" The old woman sounded really distressed. Talk flew back and forth between her and the guard. Maggie could feel Madame DuBois gesturing, but couldn't see out from under the shawl enough to know what was happening. Her foot slipped when the old woman kicked her heel, and she skidded sideways again.

The old woman pulled Maggie back from falling, and the talking ended. Claude miraculously took off at a run—in the opposite direction from the convent. Madame DuBois kept a firm hold on Maggie, but no longer kneed the back of her leg or kicked her heel.

When the sound of the guard's running feet faded into the distance, the woman let Maggie straighten up.

"Who are you! Whose side are you on? Was Simon right? What did you say to that guy—Claude—to send him on a wild goose chase?" Out of breath and out of questions, Maggie stopped talking. She hugged the long shawl close around her.

The mischievous grin that wrinkled the old woman's face made her look like a naughty little kid. "I am on your side, the side of justice, and to Claude I mentioned that the runaway child goes that way, and that I hope he catches her, because runaway girls become drunken old ladies—like you."

Maggie's mouth dropped open. "You . . . you . . . . How did you get away with it? Doesn't he know you?"

"No. I have seen him with my nephew many times. But he has not seen me. He is a criminal—like Gérard. They steal paintings."

"Gérard! He's holding Sr. Clare hostage. They plan to . . . I have to help her!" Maggie reached up to pull the shawl from her head, but Madame DuBois stopped her.

"You are shivering. Keep it. Come, I will go with you."

"No!" Maggie tried to soften her response and still think fast. "One is safer than two. I'm sure Gérard will be there, waiting for Mr. Becker to come and . . . and . . . Madame DuBois, can you go to *Hôtel La Fleur*? You know who Jean-Louis is, right? Mr. Becker captured him there. That had to have caused a big ruckus. Maybe they're still there, and you can save Jean-Louis. Call the police as soon as you can. Tell them to come to the convent. Will you do it? Please!" Maggie turned to go, then whirled back. "Thank you." She gave Madame DuBois a quick hug. "The shawl—you'll need it."

"Keep." Madame DuBois reached inside a plastic bag in her cart and pulled out a brown shawl identical to the green one she had given Maggie. "We must both go quickly now."

"Watch for Simon too, okay? We can't find him."

"I will look," Madame DuBois said, and hurried off at a shuffling trot, pushing her wire cart toward the Left Bank.

Maggie watched the old woman for the length of a deep breath, then turned and ran for the convent, her newly acquired shawl flapping against her legs.

It all seemed so unreal. What was she doing, running through a huge city in the middle of the night? All this cement. Building after claustrophobic building. Maggie's lungs tightened, and she fought for breath. How was she ever going to make it to the convent? The three blocks to go might as well be three hundred. Deep inside, she still remembered that Sr. Clare needed her, but the city was too overwhelming. Dealing with Gérard would be impossible. She had tried so hard, but now she was too tired—too scared.

Maggie's feet slowed almost to a walk, and she may have given up entirely, but for some crazy reason, Bartholomew's letter of what seemed like a hundred years ago flashed into her mind. Treat the city like a rugged mountain bike trail—was that what he had said? Fuzzy with fatigue and struggling for breath, she could hardly remember.

Dart—dodge—lift and leap. That's what she would do on a bike in the hills. Work the mud—ignore the pain. Think one step ahead of the next obstacle. That's all Gérard was—an obstacle to dodge. Panic bred energy—use it.

When Maggie arrived at the walkway across the street from the courtyard, she ducked behind a closed information kiosk and peeked carefully around the high, upright cylinder.

There he was! Still dressed completely in black, almost invisible in the mist and poor street lighting, Gérard paced outside the wall door of the courtyard. He lit one cigarette after another and kept looking across the street in Maggie's direction. If she took one step closer, she would be visible. She couldn't even reach the park entrance, only ten yards ahead on her left, without being spotted.

Her mind working fast, Maggie retraced her steps away from the church and ran all the way around the park to its far entrance. Somewhere in the back of her mind, she realized the rainy mist had stopped. No moisture covered her arms as she squeezed through the bars of the park's locked wrought-iron gate. The shawl kept catching against the iron, and she almost ditched it, but its warmth comforted her, and gave her courage. She was glad, too, for the boisterous singing that had started up inside one of the nearby coffee houses. It wasn't the full blast of Bastille Day joviality, but it was enough noise to provide a good cover.

Maggie wrapped the shawl a couple of extra times around her shoulders and raced silently across the grass to the wall that separated the park from the courtyard. As fast as she could, she scrambled up the wet slippery branches of the old gnarled tree she had painted with Sister Clare. From the tree's highest branches, she swung to the top of the cement wall, praying that Gérard would stay outside the courtyard door for another two minutes.

One more obstacle—the wrought iron fence on top of the wall. The fence was only chest-high, but the spikes at the top made it a hazardous challenge. Acquiring a few scratches in the process, Maggie eased herself over the fence to the courtyard-side of the top of the wall. Now what? It had to be a good twelve feet to the ground. A jump to the cobblestones would not only give her away, it would probably give her a broken ankle in the bargain.

Maggie hated to do it, but she draped one end of the long, finely spun shawl on a fence rod and pulled hard. The cloth gave way, making a hole that anchored the shawl to the fence spike. She had a homemade mountain-climber's rope. Her heart in her throat, she hung on for dear life and inched herself down the wall. So this is what rappelling was like. For a brief second, Maggie enjoyed her adventurous descent, but then she discovered that the length of rope ended, and she still dangled way above ground.

Trying not to panic, she hung in midair, waiting. She didn't know what it was she was waiting for until, when her strained arms couldn't hold on another second, two things happened at once.

The coffeehouse singing reached a resounding crescendo— and the shawl gave way. Maggie hit the cobblestones with a crunching thud that threw her to her hands and knees. Tiny stones bit into her flesh, and the shawl drifted down on top of her.

Biting her lip to keep from crying out against the pain, Maggie brushed the shawl from her head and, balling the cloth up in her arms, ran alongside the wall toward the crypt. One of those underground rooms held her aunt, tied and gagged.

At the top of the crypt stairs, the familiar tightness in her chest pressed the air out of Maggie's lungs, but she crept down the steps and eased the crypt door open enough for her to tiptoe inside. She hesitated. A hallway stretched ahead of her, faintly lit by an old gas lantern hanging on the wall to her right. The flickering light exposed the wood of four doors—three on her left and one just ahead of her on the right.

In the fleeting second that Maggie stood hesitating, wondering where to start looking, she felt the hair rise on her arms. Glancing nervously over her shoulder, she saw behind her, stalking soundlessly down the stairs, the outline of a human figure dressed completely in black. Maggie leaped toward the door on her right. Too late! An arm locked around her so hard, it knocked the wind out of her. A hand clapped over her mouth. She kicked and squirmed, but finally, weak from exhaustion and fear, she couldn't fight any longer. If Gérard hadn't had such a tight grip around her, she would have collapsed onto the crypt floor.

— ❧ **20** ❧ —

Time Runs Out

UNABLE TO MOVE or speak, Maggie forced herself to get angry so she wouldn't crumple. That beast Gérard!

"Alors," the night watchman growled, his lip curling into a sneer under his mustache, *"Monsieur* Becker *avait raison.* You come. *Imbecile."* Maggie kicked, twisted and turned as Gerard wrestled her down the hall and into a room on the left. Without letting up on his iron grip, he rubbed his shoulder against the wall by the door, where a light switch must be, and a single ceiling light flicked on. It was hard to see over Gerard's hairy hand plastered to her face, and the only thing Maggie could make out in the otherwise bare room was a high wooden shelf with a jumble of play equipment on it.

Gerard dragged her toward the wall that had the shelf on it and yanked her arms behind her back. She gasped in pain, and lost the only real chance she'd had to break loose. Before she could recover enough to scream, Gerard pulled a jump rope from the shelf, jerked the rope tightly around her wrists, and gagged her with a strip of the torn shawl she didn't even realize she still had.

The next thing she knew, Gerard picked her up like a sack of potatoes and dumped her into a corner of the room opposite the door. Without one look back at her, he clicked off the light and went out the door, leaving her in dank, silent darkness.

Too terrified to cry, Maggie scrunched into the dark corner, gaining what little consolation she could from the strong solidity of the walls she leaned against. The outer wall was cement. Cold. The inner dividing wall was wood. She shifted her position to lean more against its friendlier warmth. Spiders and rats hardly mattered anymore. She was so tired. Her knees and hands hurt from the fall to the cobblestones. Her head ached from the shawl stretched over her mouth.

Maggie tried to lick away the fuzzy strands of her gag. No use. The fuzz only grew in her mouth. A strangled cry rose from within her, escaping from her throat in broken pieces of sound.

She fought to control her rising panic. Fear cost too much valuable energy that she might need later. Closing her eyes and taking deep breaths through her nose, Maggie worked her way into being quiet. Only then did she realize that ever since she had been thrown into this dark cell, she had been hearing, but not hearing, intermittent moans from somewhere nearby. Sr. Clare—it had to be!

Maggie pressed herself more tightly against the corner of her prison, forcing herself into a greater stillness and straining to hear from which direction the moans were coming.

Sr. Clare sounded so weak. Tears escaped from Maggie's eyes and ran down her cheeks. She gulped down the tears and heard low moans again. Sr. Clare must be hurt! Maggie had to reach her. Had to be with her. Even if they both died, at least they would be together.

Using her feet as a lever, and the two corner walls as her balance, Maggie pushed herself inch by inch to a standing position. It seemed to take hours, but finally she made it, and groped with her bound arms along the outer cement wall toward the sound of Sr. Clare's moans.

Maggie's heart beat wild with hope as she drew closer and closer to the sound—until she hit a block she couldn't penetrate.

"Arrmmpht!" In anger and frustration, she shoved her body against another dividing wall.

How dare this hunk of wood block her from where she needed to be! Maggie lurched back, and threw herself sideways at the wall. Again. And again. Each impact produced no more than a weak thud, and the third throw beat reality into her. She slumped against the ungiving obstacle.

This was it. The end of the road. A lost battle. All the courage and strength Maggie had fought for seeped out of her. She couldn't fight a wall that had no more give to it than a . . . than a . . . ten-ton boulder. A boulder . . . A ten-ton . . .

Still slumped against the wall, Maggie shook her aching head to clear it of cobwebs. What was she trying so hard to remember?

She leaned her head against the wall, unable to think. She couldn't even hear the moans on the other side of the wall anymore—the other side of the boulder.

In the dark void of Maggie's mind the thread of a thought wove into existence. It started slowly and gained momentum. Bartholomew's letter. His words that were meant to be encouraging, but that had made her so angry at first. "Just a boulder in your path . . ." Those words had helped her once already. If only . . . yes, that was it! Maggie drew her head away from the wall and stood up straight. She shifted her hands sideways behind to try and ease the ropes that kept tightening around her wrists. This wall was no more than an obstacle to leap or dodge. Well, she couldn't leap it, so . . .

Sure of what she needed to do now, Maggie worked her way along the dividing wall until she hit a new corner, then started along what had to be the wall between her room and the hallway. She would come to the door soon.

As she moved forward, Maggie suddenly felt her arm leave the wall. For a split second she dangled at the edge of an abyss. In the next split second, she fell sideways, and slammed to a stop as abruptly as she had fallen. Pain shot through her arm, but she didn't care. She had found the door!

Quickly now, Maggie fumbled for a doorknob with her bound hands, found it, opened the door, and turned so that she was facing the hall. The moans, which she realized she hadn't heard for quite a while now, had come from the adjacent room on her right. She turned in that direction, and, leaning lightly against the wall, moved toward what she knew would soon be another door. More prepared this time, she didn't fall against the door when she found it.

Inside the new room, Maggie knew she didn't dare turn a light on, even if she could somehow manage it with her bound hands. The risk of discovery would be too great. She closed the door, faced into the room, and listened for what she hoped would come.

As soon as Sr. Clare moaned, Maggie started toward her. She moved carefully, so as not to trip over her aunt and hurt her more than she must already be. The job became harder when Sr. Clare stopped moaning again.

"Please, please, don't let her be dead." If only Maggie could keep Sr. Clare alive until the police arrived. Madame DuBois *had* to have been able to contact them by now.

Maggie shuffled along the floor, one sliding step at a time, in what she hoped was still the right direction.

Yes! Maggie's toe touched something soft, and she dropped to her knees beside her prone aunt. Awkwardly, having to do everything from behind, Maggie probed Sr. Clare's still form until she found her hands—also tied. Forced by her own tied hands to keep faced away from her aunt, Maggie had trouble maneuvering the ropes around her aunt's wrists.

The exertion of trying to free her aunt's wrists sent sweat pouring down Maggie's forehead. How could that monster of a night watchman knock her aunt out cold and still tie her up like this!

Maggie freed her aunt from her gag as well as from the ropes that had entrapped her wrists. During the process, Sr. Clare moaned twice, then retreated back into a dreadful silence.

Maggie felt desperately for her aunt's pulse. She must be alive—she was trembling. Or was it Maggie who was trembling? She took a deep breath to steady herself, and tried again to feel for Sr. Clare's pulse.

"Which room is the girl in?"

Maggie's tied hands lost their hold on her aunt's wrist, and her heart skipped a beat at the thought that the police had arrived. But she knew in the same missed heartbeat that it wasn't the police. It was Mr. Becker—right outside this room.

Whoever Mr. Becker was talking to must have gestured in response, because after a slight pause, Mr. Becker spoke again.

"You get in the van, check to make sure all the crates are there, and stay put. Keep the motor running. I'll take care of these three in short order, and I want that van moving as soon as I set foot inside it."

"*Mais, Monsieur* Becker, what . . . ?" Gérard—and he must have gestured again, because Mr. Becker answered without hesitation.

"When you get back from the airport, find Claude. The two of you can get rid of what's left of these three and get out of the country on an evening flight—exactly as planned. Now, move. We haven't got a second to waste."

What had Mr. Becker meant by "these three?" Maggie didn't have any time to think about it before the sound of Gérard's feet scuttling down the hall and up the crypt steps faded, and the door to the room opened.

Shivering uncontrollably, Maggie had to call on all the will power she possessed to shift her body so that she knelt between Sr. Clare and danger.

The door to the room swung open, and, by the hallway light, Maggie saw Mr. Becker shove Jean-Louis inside, close the door, and click on the room light.

"Jean-Louis!" His name erupted from Maggie's throat in a gurgle. The nerve of that rat, Mr. Becker! Maggie stumbled to her feet, lowered her head to turn herself into a human battering ram, and charged the enemy.

"Whoa there!" Mr. Becker stepped aside and caught Maggie by the shoulders in a grip she knew she couldn't escape.

"Mmmgghphh!"

"Maggie, listen to me—I'm not going to hurt you!" Mr. Becker kept his vice-like grip on her shoulders, but his voice softened. "Quick, Jean-Louis—take care of Thea—Sr. Clare. Maggie, I'm not the crook you think I am. It's important for all of us that you believe me. Gérard said he knocked Sr. Clare out, and from the looks of it, she's going to need help getting out of here. We don't have much time—a matter of minutes. You and Jean-Louis have got to get Sr. Clare upstairs as soon as I leave with Gérard."

Maggie's eyes widened. Jean-Louis, free of his ropes and gag, was lifting Sr. Clare into a sitting position. What was going on here? Nothing made sense anymore. Maggie stared helplessly at Jean-Louis, who murmured encouragement to Sr. Clare as he tried to rouse her and help her to her feet.

Mr. Becker was still talking. Maggie tried to concentrate on what he was saying, but all she could do was keep licking her lips with a tongue made out of used sandpaper. She wiped the back of her hand across her mouth, then lifted her hand in front of her, trying to glean some meaning out of what she had just done. Weird—why was that weird? Oh! Her gag was gone, and her hands were untied. Mr. Becker must have freed her while he was talking.

"Wrap Sr. Clare in blankets as soon as you get up to the convent,"Tanya's father was saying now. "She's suffering from shock, and I wouldn't be surprised if she has a concussion. Call a doctor as soon as possible, and after that, call the police." He scribbled something onto a page in a notebook that he pulled from his back pocket, ripped the sheet away from the notebook, and handed the paper to Maggie. "Ask for this man. Tell him I don't know where Claude is, and tell him to get here as soon as possible."

"Maggie?" It was the first time Jean-Louis had spoken since he had come into the room. "It will take two to guide *Soeur* Clare from the crypt to the presbytery."

Maggie rushed to Sr. Clare's other side and put the nun's left arm over her shoulder, the way Jean-Louis had done with her right one. Completely docile but seemingly unable to focus on what was happening, Sr. Clare let herself be led to the door.

"Mr. Becker, I don't . . ."

"Jean-Louis will explain as much to you as he knows, Maggie." Mr. Becker spoke in the gentlest voice she had ever heard him use. "For now, just get yourselves upstairs to safety, and don't go anywhere until you're sure Claude is caught or out of the country."

"But, what about Madame DuBois—this lady who's helping us. She was supposed to go to the hotel and to call the police. Where is she? Why aren't the police here already?"

Mr. Becker shook his head. "I know the lady you mean, but I don't know where she is. Home in bed, I hope—where a woman her age belongs at this hour. Tell the inspector about her when he comes."

"There is also Simon," Jean-Louis said quickly, before Mr. Becker got the door open.

"Ah, yes, Simon." A flicker of a smile crossed Mr. Becker's face. "He is safe in the hands of an agent at the airport."

Maggie's mouth fell open, and she heard Jean-Louis gasp, but they learned no more about Simon.

"If I take any longer," Tanya's father said crisply, "Gérard might come back to see what the holdup is." Mr. Becker opened the door, started out, came back. "You youngsters deserve a scolding every bit as strong as the one I'm going to give my daughter, but for right now . . ." He rubbed his hand over the emerging stubble on his chin. "I don't like to leave you—but there's no choice. It's the only way to draw attention away from you and keep things moving. Remember, give me two minutes, and get upstairs to safety."

It was scary how compliant Sr. Clare was. She stuck obediently between Maggie and Jean-Louis—a large, easily led child. No amount of nudging would speed her up, though. By the time they got to the top of the crypt stairs, Maggie's hurt shoulder ached and her nerves jangled.

"It'll take years to get her up to the apartment!" she whispered frantically to Jean-Louis. "And I'm already exhausted."

"We will stop, but only for a moment," Jean-Louis said, breathing hard. He took several deep breaths and shifted Sr. Clare's arm around his shoulders. "You are ready, Maggie?"

"Ready. At least it's getting light out here. That helps." The nun's weight settled heavier on Maggie's shoulders, and in only three steps, Maggie wished they could take another break.

"This courtyard used to be so small," she moaned, gazing down the length of the church wall. "Hoo boy, the presbytery steps look as far away as Welcome, Indiana, from here."

Maggie and Jean-Louis, Sr. Clare slung between them, took another step forward, and got pulled up short.

Until this point, Sr. Clare had been as obedient as she had been slow, but now she pulled away and took a step back toward the crypt.

"No, *Soeur* Clare!" Jean-Louis leaped after her and grabbed her arm.

Sr. Clare stopped abruptly. She looked at Jean-Louis, who let go of her arm. "What?" She paused. "Where? Oh, yes," she said vaguely, "It's morning. I must go for the *baguette.* But . . ." She brought her hand to the back of her head, touched it, and winced. "Where's my veil?" She gazed up at the pre-dawn sky above the courtyard. "'Who's on first?'"

Maggie caught her breath, and laughed uncertainly. "This does feel like a scene from 'Abbot and Costello,' doesn't it? Are you going to get better now, Sr. Clare?"

Without answering, Maggie's aunt closed her eyes for a long time. When she opened them again, she looked a lot more like herself. Maggie squirmed under Sr. Clare's gaze.

"I was terribly worried when I saw you weren't in your room, Maggie."

"Oh, Sr. Clare, I'm so sorry!" Maggie wanted to crawl under the cobblestones. "I'm really, really sorry."

Sr. Clare sighed. "At least, I can see that you're safe. What are we doing here in the courtyard?"

"*Soeur* Clare," Jean-Louis said, "we must go immediately inside to your convent. There, we will explain. Come, please." He took Sr. Clare's arm again and turned her gently back in the direction of the presbytery. Maggie came to reclaim her aunt's other arm and to continue their journey.

"I do seem dreadfully tired." Sr. Clare stopped after two steps. "Where did you say we are?" She slumped heavily between Maggie and Jean-Louis.

"Only twenty more feet to the presbytery," Maggie said desperately. "Don't give out on us now! As soon as we get in there and upstairs, you can lie down and . . ." Maggie broke off and watched in alarm as the outer wall door slowly squeaked open, seemingly of its own accord.

The door stopped halfway open and Maggie thought it must have been a gust of wind that had swung it ajar. "Jean-Louis," she whispered, looking at him around Sr. Clare, "do you think . . . ?"

Jean-Louis shook his head and motioned toward the half-open door.

From behind it, a man Maggie recognized all too well stepped into the courtyard.

— 21 —

Clamor in the Courtyard

"CLAUDE!" MAGGIE WAS sure she had never seen anybody who fit the word "sinister" so well.

"Stay where you are, and don't move!" The museum guard aimed a pistol straight at Maggie. With his free hand, he swung the courtyard door shut.

The bulk of Sr. Clare's weight shifted to Maggie's shoulders, and she struggled to hold her aunt upright as Jean-Louis let go and stepped in front of the two of them. It was a brave act, but Maggie saw that Jean-Louis' hands were trembling.

"Don't try to be a hero," Claude spat, moving slowly toward Jean-Louis. "Your life is in my hands." His heavily accented English came straight out of an old American gangster movie. "Did you think I was so dumb as not to guess that you would eventually come back here, you stupid girl? I ought to . . . wha . . . !"

Claude must not have latched the courtyard door. It banged open against the wall, and a tall, thin, man, head bent, feet churning, exploded into the courtyard. His eyes focused on a sheaf of paper in his hands, he rushed toward the presbytery.

In her heightened state of nerves, Maggie almost laughed. Jean-Louis' father and his music! He didn't even know anybody else was in the courtyard.

Claude raised his pistol. "*Arrêt!*"

The sharp command startled *Monsieur* Gagnon, and, already halfway across the courtyard, he glanced up, spotting Jean-Louis.

Maggie was glad she couldn't understand the words *Monsieur* Gagnon threw at his son as he stormed toward him with fire in his eyes. He didn't see Claude until the guard ran up to him and held the gun a foot from his nose.

"Ai-eee!" *Monsieur* Gagnon flung his arms up. The papers shot out of his hands and into the air.

Claude leaped aside from the flailing arms, and bumped into Maggie and Sr. Clare. Maggie stomped on his foot, and Sr. Clare, in an automatic move to keep him from falling, swung her arm out to grab Claude. She missed and hit his elbow.

"Arrgghh!" The gun flew out of Claude's hand.

Jean-Louis grabbed the guard around the waist and tried to wrestle him to the ground, but Claude broke free, and smashed him with his fist. Jean-Louis reeled backward, his hands to his face.

"*Mon fils!*" *Monsieur* Gagnon flew at Claude, swinging wildly. Words and fists beat at the startled crook.

Maggie ran for the dropped gun. Heavy and cold, it needed both hands to hold it. She thought fast. Without his gun, Claude was next to harmless against her, Jean-Louis and his dad, but she couldn't risk running around everyone to throw the thing in the dumpster. What then?

A picture of Annie Oakley shooting playing cards thrown into the air in Buffalo Bill's Wild West Show fell into Maggie's mind. If that rifle-toting, sharp-shooting cowgirl could do it, Maggie could too.

"Everybody hold it right there!" In the confusing din of *Monsieur* Gagnon yelling and beating at Claude with both fists and feet, Sr. Clare trying to part them, and Jean-Louis stumbling forward to try and help his father, nobody seemed to hear her. "Hold it, I say!"

Maggie lifted the heavy pistol above her head. Holding onto it with both hands and pointing it skyward, she cocked the hammer with her thumb and jerked the trigger. The unexpected recoil and explosion sent her reeling backward. She regained her balance in time to see Jean-Louis, his father and Claude spring apart, and Sr. Clare stumble aside. They stared open-mouthed at her.

Maggie zeroed her aim in on Claude. "Stay right where you are, you thief. And put your hands behind your back." Maggie stuck to her Annie Oakley persona. "This here is classified as a deadly weapon, and I just proved I know how to use it." What a lie. She hoped the museum guard couldn't see how her knees trembled.

All eyes but Maggie's swiveled to face the wall door behind her, and she risked a quick glance over her shoulder.

Two uniformed and armed *gendarmes* stepped into the court-yard from outside. The tree branches above the park wall rustled, and another *gendarme* appeared head-and-shoulders above the wall Maggie had climbed over only a few hours earlier.

Good old Madame DuBois, Maggie thought. She *had* gotten hold of the police. But, what had taken them so long?

Jean-Louis, his eye already swelling shut, spoke rapidly to the *gendarmes* on the ground. One of them pulled out a pair of handcuffs and snapped them around Claude's wrists. Without his weapon, the guard seemed to have lost all his bluster, and he gave no resistance.

The other *gendarme* on the ground came over to Maggie, and she realized, finally, that it was all over. They were safe. The policeman's weathered face swam before her. So long, Annie Oakley.

Maggie managed to switch the gun around and turn it over to the *gendarme,* handle first, before everything went starry-black and she felt herself falling.

22

The Last Pieces of the Puzzle

EARLY WEDNESDAY morning—a little more than forty-eight hours after Annie Oakley bit the dust, Maggie eased herself down to sit on the courtyard steps outside the presbytery. She had slept the rest of Monday away until suppertime. Then, after a shower and Sr. Germaine's insistence on paying some attention to her scraped knees and hands, Maggie had slept all night Monday, rested yesterday, and slept the night through again last night. She was downright slept out.

The early sun's rays felt good on her uplifted face, and the courtyard seemed different from before. Peaceful. No Gérard to yell at her. No Claude to threaten her. No more policemen to question her. The red geraniums looked fresh and perky in their flower box by the presbytery steps. This should be a perfect morning, if only . . .

Maggie's body stiffened at the sight of the wall door opening, and she let her breath out in a whoosh when she saw that it was Jean-Louis.

"*Bonjour,* Maggie."

She winced. "I was hoping you'd come over, but your eye! It looks as though you've been at the wrong end of a heavy-weight boxing match."

"*Mais, non.* This is a very good thing that has happened." Jean-Louis moved across the courtyard in his sea-captain gait. "Because of what happened to my eye, my father is different. Did you see how he acted when Claude hit me?" A look of

172

wonder lit Jean-Louis' face. "He had to guide me to our home that morning, because I had trouble with seeing. In our kitchen, he put cold cloths on my eye. He was very gentle."

Jean-Louis sat beside Maggie on the steps, his lame leg stretched out before him. He stared at it in awe. "This morning, my father was at first silent, as he usually is, but then he spoke directly to me. He said that it looks as though I am doing well with walking, in spite of this leg. He asked me how my eye feels, and said that perhaps we will go to a concert together soon. He has, I think, forgiven himself for being the cause of my accident. I am very happy with my black eye. Have you talked with your mother or father yet?"

"No." Maggie grimaced at the pain that shot through her knees when she pulled up her legs and wrapped her arms around them. That made the shoulder she had used to attack the crypt wall between herself and Sr. Clare twinge too. What a mess she was! The part of her that hurt the most, though, was inside. "Sr. Germaine said Mom called yesterday morning, when I was asleep, but she didn't say much, I guess, except that she would be in touch. Yeesh, I might as well drop out of existence, as far as she and Bartholomew are concerned!"

Maggie quickly changed the topic. "When I turned that gun over to the gendarme, I fainted like a pink-cheeked extra in *Gone With the Wind!*" She laughed half-heartedly, and dropped the pretense of humor. "Yesterday, in between naps, I tried to phone home myself, but nobody answered. Between late morning and nighttime, I tried five times. Nobody was home at the Beckers', either. Maybe they all went out partying together— wouldn't that be a miracle? I still don't know if anything has changed between Bartholomew and Mr. Becker. Why doesn't somebody call?" Too near tears to go on, Maggie stopped talking.

"Maggie? I am thinking . . ."

Maggie never found out what Jean-Louis was thinking right then. The courtyard door opened for the second time that morning, to reveal Sr. Germaine standing out on the sidewalk, holding a big cardboard box.

"We have people who have brought some donations for us," the little golden nun said. "Will you help me with the other things outside the door, Maggie? Jean-Louis, will you take this box?"

He was already on his feet and moving toward her.

"Maggie?" Sr. Germaine tilted her head, waiting.

It wasn't that Maggie didn't want to help. It was just that her knees and shoulder hurt. Her head ached. She felt sluggish. What was a bunch of people doing, coming so early, anyway? And what was the strange look that appeared on Jean-Louis' face when he stepped outside the courtyard and took the box from Sr. Germaine? Maggie rose and limped toward him and Sr. Germaine. As she approached the open door, Jean-Louis stepped to one side, Sr. Germaine to the other.

"What is this—an honor guard?" Maggie turned from one to the other. "How many boxes are there, anyway? I bet . . . ." Her eyes opened wider than the door had.

"It can't be—ohhh!" She threw her arms out to her mother, who had dropped her suitcase and was running toward her. After a long, blissful hug, Maggie pulled away and turned to Bartholomew, who stood on the sidelines watching. Maggie hesitated, uncertain.

"Maggie, darlin'." He broke into his wide-as-the-Yukon grin and engulfed her in a bear hug that lifted her off her feet as he swung her around. "You *are* still in one piece! Richard assured us you were, but we had to see for ourselves to believe it. Your mother had an intuition. 'There's something wrong with Maggie—I know it,' she said Sunday night after she tried to reach you. "'I know I may have made a mistake on the time, and it might be midnight in Paris,' she said, 'but, I still think there's something wrong.' Never argue with a mother's intuition." Bartholomew put Maggie down and drew Mara into the circle of his arms.

"Sunday afternoon, when Sr. Thérèse said the youngsters were out touring before going to supper with Richard and Tanya— that sounded okay. But Monday afternoon," Bartholomew said to Sr. Germaine and Jean-Louis, "when Sr. Thérèse answered again and told us Maggie was napping, and so was Thea, we knew for sure something had to be wrong. Neither Maggie nor Thea *ever* sleep that much.

"We sat around trying to figure out what might be going on when, the next thing we knew, Richard was calling from Paris. He told us what had happened and offered us a honeymoon here so we could come and see for ourselves that Maggie and Thea were all right. We already know Tanya is okay."

Right on cue, a beautiful, black-haired gremlin stepped out from behind a tree in the park and pushed open the wrought iron park gate.

"Tanya! You are the *limit!* Did you stay in Paris too?"

"Yep. I would have come over to see you before this, but Dad told me I had to let you rest. Pity, you could have come shopping with me. It's okay, though. Now we can all go. Look!"

Two more figures appeared from behind the tree. Mrs. Becker's face glowed, and even Mr. Becker smiled.

"Oh, my astonished countenance!" Maggie clasped her hands to the sides of her head. "Jean-Louis, can you imagine?"

Sr. Germaine hustled everybody up the stairs, where they crowded into the kitchen and perched on breakfast stools or stood, leaning against counters. Sr. Clare, still looking pale, joined them, and Jean-Louis brought her a dining room chair. She stayed up way longer than the doctor would have said she should, but she said she couldn't bear to miss the fun.

"I'm feeling much better," she insisted. "I'm sure the doctor would consider this good therapy." Her resemblance to Bartholomew seemed to grow stronger in his presence. Her eyes sparkled the way his did, her smile broadened, and her gestures grew more like his—expansive and all-inclusive. Maggie couldn't take her gaze away from the two of them.

"Hello, you old troublemaker," Sr. Clare said to Mr. Becker. "I don't know whether to thank you for saving me, or scold you for getting me into this mess in the first place."

"I owe you an apology." Mr. Becker took Sr. Clare's hand in his, and turned to Bartholomew. "I owe you one too."

Bartholomew shook his head, but Mr. Becker stopped him. "No, its important that everyone hear this. I have regretted more than I can say, Bartholomew, for making things so difficult for you and your new family. I'd been working on this case for three years, Maggie." Still holding Sr. Clare's hand, he turned and spoke directly to Maggie.

"When Bartholomew came to Welcome—capable, knowledgeable about art, his sister's American representative—I feared he would sense something and go to the police. It would have blown years of hard work and sabotaged the whole case. I was afraid he was already suspicious about my inviting Thea—Sr. Clare—to give a show."

At the word "suspicious", Tanya gasped, but Maggie and Jean-Louis grinned triumphantly at each other. They had guessed right! Mr. Becker's scrawled note had meant that he was worried about Bartholomew being suspicious of *him*. Maggie had to struggle to listen to the rest of what Mr. Becker was saying.

"I couldn't afford to let Bartholomew close enough to get really suspicious and cause everything to cave in on us," he said, still directing his words to Maggie, "not when we were finally so close to winding it up. I'm not sorry I kept Bartholomew at a distance, but I'm very sorry to have caused you, Maggie, and all of you, so much unhappiness."

Grief—or was it relief—filled Maggie's eyes with tears. She wiped them away quickly. "Gérard and Claude weren't really very smart, were they?" she said.

Mr. Becker shook his head. "No, thank heavens. They're small-time gambling buddies who lost more than they could afford. Claude's been a part of the smuggling ring for years, and he knew about Gérard's need to pay off some king-sized debts. He told Gérard about the job here at the church, and when I came over to make the exhibit invitation to Sr. Clare, I offered Gérard a sum he couldn't refuse to act as the inside man here."

Mr. Becker smiled briefly. "Sr. Clare helped too, when she so willingly accepted Gérard's offer to make the shipping crates for her. That made it easy to sneak the stolen paintings into her crates. It took a long time to set all that up, and not even I had a clue that Gerard's aunt had gotten suspicious of his behavior and had started tailing him. Of course, we didn't know about you two, either." Mr. Becker gently let go of Sr. Clare's hand and frowned at Maggie and Jean-Louis.

"You nearly got yourselves and Thea killed with your detective antics—and almost thwarted this case at a crucial moment."

His frown eased up a little. "You did do some good sleuthing, though. I have to admit that. The piece of wood you found fits the broken Dumolin frame perfectly."

"Your friend Simon, however, has a few things to learn if he's going to do any more detective work. For one thing, he should tuck his shirttail in when he hides behind trees to make sketches. He also needs to concentrate harder on his detecting than he does on his sketching. I shook him in thirty seconds after leaving the art gallery, and the agent I had tailing him after that caught him at the airport easier than a squirrel can catch a fallen nut. She locked him up in the storage room to keep him safe— and to protect the sketches he made. They're invaluable pieces of evidence."

"I can't believe all the action I missed!" Tanya cried. "You kept me cooped up in that old hotel room my whole time in Paris."

"There was good reason for that, young lady."

Maggie squirmed at the stern set of Mr. Becker's square jaw. Tanya didn't squirm, though. She met the stubborn set of his eyes with a daring defiance that wobbled only at the end.

"You will let me go on the boat tour with Jean-Louis and Maggie tonight, won't you?"

The struggle showed clearly on Mr. Becker's strong face.

"Dad, this is Paris! It's Maggie's birthday outing! You can stick the summer court martial back on me when we get home."

Mr. Becker rubbed his hand over his chin, and Maggie could tell he wasn't unaware of his wife's silent plea.

"Go," he said at last. "It'll be good for you. Maybe I've held the reins a little too tight. You'll be in good company, anyway."

"Hey, speaking of good company . . ." Maggie turned to Jean-Louis. "Madame DuBois is the real hero of this outfit—waking up in the hospital just in time to get the police here to nab Claude. Maybe she and Simon can come with us tonight too."

"Simon, maybe, but the answer to Madame DuBois is 'no,'" Sr. Clare spoke up before Jean-Louis could get a word out. "That poor woman has had enough nighttime excursions lately to last a lifetime, and if she falls off another curb and knocks herself out again, it could be the end of her. She's coming for supper. That'll be plenty of excitement for today. She's only been out of the hospital for twenty-four hours, and she is eighty-three, after all."

Maggie's mouth dropped open. "Well. Well, now. Bowl me over with a feather duster. I kind of knew she was older than . . . well, you know. She doesn't act old, so I forgot. Yep, we'll have to take Madame DuBois on a daytime trip. I haven't seen Simon since we got him into so much trouble, but I bet he'll come with us tonight."

Maggie was right. That evening, leaning over the railing on the upper deck of their tour boat, Simon told Maggie, Jean-Louis and Tanya what had happened at the airport on Sunday morning.

"Gérard walked right into the trap. I saw him getting put into the police van, and the funny thing was, he looked relieved. Maybe a good, long time in prison will be kind of restful after all he's been through." Simon scratched the back of his head. "The agent who caught me suggested I get a job sketching people at trials and stuff. You know, make those kinds of pictures they put in the papers and news magazines? 'Good pay,' she said. I told her, 'not a chance. I'm done with anything related to crooks, courts and detectives!' Give me the life of a peaceful sidewalk artist and Mètro singer any day. I like knowing that when I sit down at a café table to drink a cup of coffee, that's all I'll . . ."

"Simon!" Maggie put her hand over his mouth at the same time that Jean-Louis said,

"If you do not stop talking, you will never have time to draw or sing again!"

"Don't worry, they're just teasing." Tanya slid her hand into the crook of Simon's arm and moved closer to him.

Maggie and Jean-Louis bent back to look at each other around them. Jean-Louis crossed his eyes, and Maggie laughed. Then she sighed happily and turned back to relish the view of Paris by night. A city really could be beautiful, she thought. But even better than that, she wasn't going to lose Tara after all.

"Hey," said Tanya, interrupting Maggie's thoughts. "I know what let's do. Let's get off at the next stop and take our own tour of Paris. I want to see all the most exciting spots. If we get hungry, I've still got Dad's credit card. We can travel in style!"

Maggie's heart sank under an old, familiar weight, then, surprisingly, lifted. A few short weeks ago, she would have cringed at Tanya's suggestion but would have tagged along—hating herself for giving in to her friend's whim, yet too wishy-washy to refuse. But Maggie realized all at once that Paris had changed her.

"Oh, no you don't," she said firmly. "Jean-Louis and Simon and I will show you some great places, but we won't need your dad's credit card."

"At the end of our boat tour, we will take you to the first great place," Jean-Louis promised. "Shakespeare and Company Bookshop."

"Right," Maggie agreed. "Shakespeare may be 'out' for the summer in Welcome, but he's 'in' in Paris, the neatest city I've ever known. Look!"

Le Bateau Mouche slowly floated along the Seine, past the golden-lit Notre Dame Cathedral and the sparklingly intricate Eiffel Tower. Maggie stopped talking and leaned on the ship's railing with Jean-Louis, Simon and Tanya to soak in the incredible view. Without moving away from the railing, but using only her legs and feet, she broke into a spontaneous tap sequence, dancing the light-hearted rhythm that beat so strongly within her.

Historic Note

Notre-Dame des Blancs-Manteaux (Our Lady of the White Cloaks) is located in downtown Paris. It was first occupied in 1258 by the Serfs of Mary, a group of monks who wore white cloaks.

In the 17th century, the Guillemites, an offshoot of the Benedictine Order, replaced the Serfs of Mary. After the Guillemites came the community of St. Germain des Prés.

What is now the present-day church was begun in 1685, and renovations for the adjacent convent were begun.

In 1792, several buildings were destroyed, and what was left was formed into a parish in 1802.

Today, in the 21st century, Notre-Dame des Blancs-Manteaux remains a parish church, and the children of the parish do, indeed, have their gatherings in the spare rooms of the crypt. Coming in and out through the tiny cobblestone courtyard, they pass right by the ancient tree that grows on the park side of the wall, with its branches that extend over the wall to the church side.

Also true to life, the secret stairway in the presbytery is located between the walls, just as Maggie and Jean-Louis found it. It was originally used by the monks for "night duty," serving as a quiet passageway for a monk to check the monastery at night to see if all was well without disturbing the other monks. It was also the only access to the bell tower.

As for the rest of the presbytery, it, too, stands as Maggie knew it, except for some minor changes made for clarity.

The general location of the church within the city is accurate also. You would be able to find it quite easily.

If you wished to stay in Hôtel La Fleur, though, you would be unable to find it where it should be on the West Bank. Many other old and quaint, new and luxurious hotels can be found in that area, but Hôtel La Fleur is entirely fictional.

However, the other landmarks in the story, such as Notre Dame Cathedral, the Shakespeare and Company Bookstore, and the bridges over the Seine are all there to be seen and enjoyed whenever you make a visit to this historic and compelling city.

About the Author

Echo Lewis, a member of Madonna House Apostolate, a Roman Catholic Community with its central house located in Combermere, Ontario, Canada, has been writing short stories and books for children for several years. Some of her stories have appeared in various American and Canadian periodicals, but her previous books have all been written, hand bound, and sold through the Madonna House Mission Shop in Combermere. *A Long Way from Welcome* is her first professionally published novel.